JUNKYARD
BARGAIN

Books by Faith Hunter

The Jane Yellowrock Series
SKINWALKER
BLOOD CROSS
MERCY BLADE
RAVEN CURSED
DEATH'S RIVAL
BLOOD TRADE
BLACK ARTS
BROKEN SOUL
DARK HEIR
SHADOW RIGHTS
COLD REIGN
THE JANE YELLOWROCK WORLD COMPANION
DARK QUEEN
SHATTERED BONDS
TRUE DEAD
FINAL HEIR

Compilations
BLOOD IN HER VEINS
OF CLAWS AND FANGS

continued...

The Soulwood Series
BLOOD OF THE EARTH
CURSE ON THE LAND
FLAME IN THE DARK
CIRCLE OF THE MOON
SPELLS FOR THE DEAD
RIFT IN THE SOUL

The Rogue Mage Series
BLOODRING
SERAPHS
HOST
THE ROGUE MAGE RPG PLAYERS HANDBOOK
THE ROGUE MAGE RPG GAME MASTER'S GUIDE

Anthologies
TRIALS (e-book)
TRIBULATIONS (e-book)
TRIUMPHANT (Omnibus of TRIALS and TRIBULATIONS)

The Junkyard Cats Series
JUNKYARD CATS
JUNKYARD BARGAIN
JUNKYARD WAR
JUNKYARD ROADHOUSE (2024)

JUNKYARD BARGAIN

novella 2

FAITH HUNTER

JUNKYARD BARGAIN
ISBN 978-1-62268-176-1
Copyright © 2021 Faith Hunter

All rights reserved, including the right to reproduce this book or portions thereof in any form whatsoever. For more information contact Lore Seekers Press, P.O. Box 4251 CRS, Rock Hill, SC 29732. Or online at www.loreseekerspress.com

This book is a work of fiction. Names, characters, places and incidents are products of the author's imagination or are used fictitiously. Any resemblance to actual events, locales, or persons, living or dead, is entirely coincidental.

Also available in e-book form: ISBN 978-1-62268-164-8

Cover illustration by Rebecca Frank, Bewitching Book Covers.

Printed in the United States of America on acid-free paper.

Lore Seekers Press is an imprint of Bella Rosa Books.
Lore Seekers Press and logo are trademarks of Bella Rosa Books.

10   9   8   7   6   5   4   3   2   1

Acknowledgments

No book is written in a vacuum. This novella, and the entire Junkyard Cats series, has been dependent on several people.

Editor Steve Feldberg at Audible for all the wonderful suggestions and insights for the Audible Original. Every care has been taken to deviate not at all.

Agent Lucienne Diver with The Knight Agency for acquiring an Audible Original for the Junkyard Cats series.

Cover design by Rebecca Frank of Bewitching Book Covers. Love it!

Robert Martin, physicist and theoretical physicist-adventurer. The creator of the science behind the WIMP engines and the EntNu communications system in the Junkyard Universe.

Bonnie Smietanowska, physicist.

Mud Mumudes for all things plant-ish and genetic-y.

Brenda Rezk for breaking down genetic stuff I couldn't understand.

William Joseph Roberts aka Hillbilly for biker club info.

Teri Lee Akar editor extraordinaire.

Let's Talk Promotions for running PR.

And to Lore Seekers Press for the e-book and print editions, thank you.

JUNKYARD BARGAIN

Buck Harlan—my friend, the closest thing I had left to a father—was dead because of me.

Dead protecting me.

My first thought in the morning, every morning.

Before coffee. Before breakfast. Every. Single. Morning.

His face, half eaten away by a swarm of genetically modified ants. His Outlaw Militia Warrior tattoos left untouched. The note warning me, clutched in his fingers.

I deliberately recalled everything, including tossing a half-empty gallon of Maltodine into the old Tesla fuselage, the vehicle that delivered Harlan. The accelerant burned his body to ash, obliterated the mutated ants that were eating him, and destroyed any evidence that might suggest I had killed my only friend in the world.

I studied his face, the position of his fingers, in my memory. Every detail was seared into my soul like a prayer for vengeance. The memories of death and debts owed.

I stared at the ceiling of my office, the smooth metal alloy reflecting the faint lights. So many secrets to hide. And three things to do: carry on my father's legacy, keep myself hidden from the people who would try to use me, and take revenge on Harlan's killers.

The weight of all that was heavy, even this early, still in my bed, and my memory darted back to Pops shouting to get me up in the mornings after Little Mama died and the war still raged. "Get your ass outta bed, Little Girl! We got PRC to kill!" Every morning.

The smell of coffee was fresh and potent in the filtered air, the trickle of water into the pot what awakened me. Coffee meant work, weapons to obtain, weapons that could take down my enemy—the queen who killed Harlan and sent his body to me, then followed it here to Smith's Junk and Scrap and attacked me and mine.

I had won that first battle, but if I waited until that queen, Clarisse Warhammer, attacked me again, I would end up as dead as Harlan. I needed to go to war against her and her thralls. Soon. As soon as I had possession of the weapons to make victory possible. As soon as I found her nest, I'd go to war. For Harlan.

Satisfied that I had done my daily penance, I climbed out of bed. It was two hours before dawn, in the cool perfection of a desert morning, and I had work to do. I let the two cat queens of the junkyard prides out of the airlocks, used the waterless personal toilette compartment, yawned, scratched my fingernails through my short hair, and smeared on the first layer of moisturizers and sunscreens.

I sniffed my work clothes from the day before yesterday and decided they weren't too rank, so I pulled them on. Draping clothes across hot scrap metal in the midday sun helped to make the stench bearable, though nothing got rid of stains and sweat stink like detergent and water. But water was pricy. I lived quarter-to-quarter, which meant I was always broke. Decent now, I poured a cup of coffee and turned to face the airlock hatch, waiting.

Exactly five minutes and fifteen seconds after I rolled from bed, Cupcake tapped on the office door. Just like every morning. After the first couple of mornings, I figured she had learned how to access the chrono and the supply inventory functions of the office to better serve me, so she could get here with my food faster. I hated losing my morning private time, but I hadn't figured out what to do with my unwanted guest, and Cupcake needed to be useful. A thrall's desire to please was a little like having a dog that needed to herd, or fetch, or guard. Cupcake needed a job, and when I didn't give her one, she gave herself one. She had taken over half the meal prep and gardening from Mateo. She cleaned my living area. She had begun organizing the business's financial records. She was making a detailed map of the property and what scrap was where. She was organizing everything. She was driving me crazy.

I pressed a small spot on the command board to unlock the hatch and said, "Come."

Cupcake entered through the outer, then inner, airlock doors, backing in with a breakfast tray. "Good morning, Sunshine!" she called. "We have pancakes with stevia, an MRE of fake scrambled eggy goo made with habanero peppers, and roasted beets with garlic. And you got a package in the mail! Look!" She waved a padded brown envelope that crinkled from the pressure of her fingers.

I held in a sigh and a curse. Cupcake was one of those repulsive morning people, and when I didn't appreciate her efforts, she was also weepy. She was mentally and emotionally geared to ruin my morning, every morning, and nothing I had done except stay silent had stopped her tears.

"It smells kinda funky, but it sat in the hot mailbox all day yesterday," she informed me, smiling happily, the envelope and flimsy hemp-paper fliers in one hand, the tray in the other.

"Funky how?" I asked, sniffing the air. The only thing I smelled was the habaneros and garlic.

"Rotten meat funky," she said, waving it again.

My eyes landed on the envelope.

Cupcake placed the food tray and mail on the dinette bench, snapped open a tablecloth, and unloaded the china and sterling silver onto the cheap laminated table. I had no idea which outer shed she had raided for the expensive fancy dinnerware and the sterling, but on the final day of her transitioning to a thrall, I was eating off fancy porcelain. "Sit, sit, sit, sit, sit," she said, holding out the package. Gingerly, I accepted it, and caught a whiff of stink.

In dark blue marker was my name. My real name. Shining Smith, care of Smith's Junk and Scrap, Near Naoma, West Virginia. Accurate as far as addresses went in the post-World War III world. Too accurate.

I held the package away from me as if it would explode if I moved. Because it might.

Staring at the envelope, I placed my mug on the table, and sat as Cupcake put a linen square across my lap. She brought more coffee.

"I'm betting we'll have broccoli coming up in a week or so," she chattered, "and soon we'll have *watermelon*." Which was difficult but not impossible in a desert greenhouse. She plopped down, sitting across from me at the repurposed RV dinette.

Carefully, I tore open the envelope, and the stench flooded into the room. Rotten meat for real. Gently, I pulled out the crinkly old bubble wrap. Bubble wrap wasn't made anymore, not anywhere, but there were tons of the old stuff, and it was used to ship delicate things like jewelry. But this bubble wrap was damp and sticky, coated inside with a wet brown residue.

Cupcake asked, "Shining? Don't you like the breakfast?"

I looked at her and knew my eyes were too big. She didn't seem to care about the reek, but I hadn't eaten her offering, and that was bad.

"What's wrong?" she asked, those blasted tears gathering. Cupcake had probably always been emotionally fragile. The original transition to thrall, forced on her by Warhammer to create a servant he could use, had weakened her, and my forced transition—to save her life—only made that instability worse. I was careful around her, not wanting to wound her more.

"I'm good." Thinking back over her last words, I asked softly, "Watermelon?"

"I love me some watermelon," she said brightly, and launched into a monologue about the various kinds. I lowered the damp, stinking bubble wrap below the table edge and peeled back the tape holding it together. It released and opened like a crinkly noxious flower.

Inside was a finger. A human finger.

Electric shock cascaded through me, igniting every nerve ending. I slid the napkin off my lap to the bench seat and placed the bubble wrap and finger on it. Studied it. Couldn't take my eyes off it.

It had a rounded nail, painted with the remnants of purple polish. It was slightly stubby, hairless, and had been clipped off with something like gardener's snips if the end was any indication. She had been alive when it was cut. There had been a lot of blood, and it hadn't been washed off.

"You need to eat. That eggy stuff isn't good when it gets cold."

I looked at Cupcake, seeing her as I seldom bothered to. She was forty-two, blond, curvy, and prematurely wrinkled and deeply tanned as most Old Ladies are, from riding bitch seat behind their biker mademen. When she came to me, injured and near death, she had been hard-bitten and angry, but the transition had softened everything, including her mental acuity and her ability to handle stress. It made sense. She had been infected with bio-nanobots from her own queen. Then with my even weirder ones. My nanos were probably still doing battle inside her, still changing her immune system, brain, and body, down to the genetics.

Her tears spilled over. I had upset her. Again. I didn't know what to do with Cupcake. She didn't know what to do with herself. I had no idea how to keep her happy because all she wanted to do was work and serve me, her queen, like a worker ant in a hive-nest.

I wiped my fingers and lifted the fork. Carried some mushy eggy stuff to my mouth. It didn't need to be chewed, was barely palatable, and only then because it was full of hot peppers and salt, but the yellow slop was protein, and no one wasted protein. I swallowed, despite the rotten stench rising from the seat beside me. Still beneath the tabletop, one-handed, I rolled the finger into the bubble wrap and my napkin. I needed to run diagnostics on it for identification, but not while Cupcake was in here. I quickly finished the peppery goo.

"I love broccoli," I said, shoveling beets into my mouth. "I had broccoli pesto once. It's good."

"Oh my *god*, yes. Anything with garlic and pine nuts is good. You ever tried Brussels sprouts pesto? *So good!* The greenhouse is just blooming up a storm," she nattered on now that I had contributed to the conversation, once again cheery, her blue eyes sparkling. I ate and heard her say, "That new hemp mesh Mateo and I strung up? The stuff that was left over from shading the greenhouse compound? We put it up on aisle Tango three."

"Mmm," I said, now scooping in the pancakes. Trying not to puke at the growing rotten-finger stench.

"This place needs a good cleaning," she said. "It's getting kinda rank in here."

"Right. Soon. New hemp mesh?" I reminded her.

"It's absorbing and capturing moisture out of the night air like a dream. Come winter, we might bring in enough to actually get a shower once a week."

That caught my attention. I swigged my coffee so I could talk. She poured me more. "Fresh water?" I asked.

"Nearly a week's supply for drinking and watering the greenhouse, in a little over ten days," she said, pouring herself a cup of coffee. "We think we can do twice that in winter."

My hand, holding the fancy fork, halted halfway to my mouth. "That's . . . That's really good."

"It's not a full replacement, yet," she prattled, "but not bad for summer, and if Mateo and I can get that water tower off the office roof and patch it up, we'll have a good place to store water."

Something like pleasure, maybe mixed with joy, flowed through me—a rare and unexpected sensation. "I'm . . . I'm proud of you, Cupcake."

Cupcake's blue eyes widened. Her color went high as she blossomed at the praise. "Eat," she ordered, pointing at my meal, shaking with elation.

I didn't praise her enough. I had to remember to do that. I ate. The buckwheat and millet pancakes were tasty enough. The roasted beets were surprisingly sweet and tender.

"It's good."

She hid her smile in her coffee cup. That was the thing about thralls. They were eager to please, *needed* to please, quite literally might die if they couldn't find a way to serve and didn't get attention from their nanobot-donor queen. She set down her cup, whipped a nail file out of her pocket, and reached for my left hand. "Not this morning," I said softly. To keep her from freezing in uncertainty, I continued, "Tell me more about the netting and the free water." Then, because it made her glow, I added, "This is exciting."

I spent nearly half of Smith's Junk and Scrap's profits on drinking water, and adding Cupcake to my expenses had already ruined this quarter's budget. Since the Russians exploded WIMP bombs over Germany that punched a short-term hole in the magnetosphere, tore away the ozone layer, and wrecked the atmosphere, rain was a rarity everywhere, especially in the West Virginia desert. I usually got a shower only when I went into Naoma for supplies.

Cupcake talked nonstop through the rest of my breakfast about the water collection device and the long list of plant varieties she was planning. Finally, Cupcake wound down and said brightly, "I'll feed the cats and get Mateo to bring the skids with our trade goods up to the entrance so we can pack the truck. I'm excited about our trip. It'll be fun!"

Fun. Not the word I'd choose for a dangerous mission to gather the weapon we needed to kill Warhammer. "Good," I lied.

She swept her blonde hair to the side, like a teenager. "Can I help you pack?"

"I'm packed." She looked skeptical, so I added, "I packed the dress you insisted on." I kept several duffels ready to go. All I had to dump in were the IDs and the toiletries for each trip's purpose.

"I'll bring the truck up, then. I did a full eval on the electronics and a mech assessment yesterday. We're ready to go."

I stared at her. "You do evaluations and assessments?" That was new.

"Mateo loaned me one of his Berger chips. Once I plugged in the info, it was a piece of cake." Briskly, she gathered up my dirty dishes and placed them in the sink where she wiped them with a rag and spritzed them with cleanser before leaving them to dry, the citrusy scent almost overriding the rotten-meat smell. She grabbed the tray and the tablecloth one-handed, carried kibble out the inner airlock, and rattled cat food into the metal pans before opening the outer airlock. I heard eager cat sounds as they came running. Cupcake closed the inner airlock and left me alone.

A little nauseated from the stench, I carried the bubble-wrapped finger to the med-bay, opened the hood, and set the unit to T.O.D and C.O.D—time of death and cause of death—and Identify. I could have used the portable viber, but I needed more info than it would provide.

I closed the clear plasticized med-bay hood, started the process, and waited. The finger was small and bloody and dead. I had no actual proof yet, but the finger delivery had to be related to Harlan and his death. I'd taken out most of Warhammer's no-longer-human nest, but she and her primary mate had gotten away. I couldn't let that stand. As soon as I had the weapons and the location, I was going to war. Part of that would be a complicated, dangerous, and beyond expensive fight-my-way-through-to-Charleston expedition.

If this finger belonged to the person I feared it did, I was going to have to adjust my plans, incorporate a rescue into the war, and move up my timetable, fast.

The med-bay dinged. On the screen, I read the name I had been fearing: Captain Evelyn Raymond, second-in-command of the USSS *SunStar*.

"Bloody damn," I whispered. I fell onto the dinette seat and put my head on the old laminated tabletop. "*Damndamndamn.*" I sucked in air against my anger, wishing I hadn't promised Pops I'd never say *fuck*. It would be so satisfying right now. "*Damndamn-Bloody* . . . Gaaah!" I raised my head and stared, unseeing, into my living space, breathing through the fury and frustration. As Mateo and I had long feared, Clarisse had captured Evelyn Raymond. We had to rescue her.

I rested my head on the cheap tabletop until my temper cooled, sat upright, blew out a breath, and centered myself. I envisioned Tuffs, the original queen and Guardian Cat of the Junkyard Cats. Within seconds, Tuffs and her court were at the inner airlock, chasing all the hungry cats away, claiming territory.

I let in the cats and they raced everywhere, exploring. Tuffs brought a different batch each time she came to visit, the Guardian Cat making sure all her pride members knew the layout of the office and where the food was kept. I also knew that if I somehow died, they would devour my body until there was nothing left but bones and teeth. They had feasted on human flesh. They liked it.

Tuffs jumped onto the table and sat. I retook my place across from her and lowered my head. She put her head against mine. We didn't *have* to touch to communicate, but it helped. I sent a picture vision of our heads touching, followed by a picture vision of the world as viewed from the front gate, looking away from the junkyard. Then a picture vision of a big truck rolling down the road in a cloud of dust, me driving and Spy, a pride member, sitting on the dash. Last, I sent one of my head and Spy's touching.

Tuffs reared back and said, *Sisssss*, hissing at me, showing her teeth, saying in her very pissed-off cat-speak, *No!*

I had been afraid of that. Spy would not be joining our mission.

The sun wasn't up yet when I stepped into the cool West Virginia air, tapped my comms, and said, "Mateo. Got a minute?"

"Bad news or worse?" his bio-metallic larynx ground out.

"Eh. Could be worse, but not by much. It's Evelyn."

Mateo didn't answer right away, the silence between us the smooth background quiet of EntNu communications, courtesy of the USSS *SunStar*'s comms.

Over the connection, I heard the faint whining movement of servos and the even softer sound of a warbot's foot-pegs touching down in sequence—Mateo in stealth mode, approaching my position.

Three junkyard cats raced out of the darkness and sprang up onto piles of scrap metal, curious, watching in the darkness. Waiting. *Hhhhah mmm*, one of them said. That meant *yes,* or *this is true,* or *this is good* in cat-speak. I figured they were expecting entertainment. Maybe a human version of a catfight? Me and Mateo? He'd squish me like a bug. And the cats would get protein. *That* would explain their excitement.

Mateo had gone down with the *SunStar*. He had thought he was the only one on board when the battleship plunged out of the sky during an intra-system clash with the Chinese, the Russians, and the Bugs—the aliens "visiting" Earth. Only recently had we figured out that Mateo's second-in-command, Captain Evelyn Raymond, had still been on board the *SunStar*, in direct contradiction of orders, backing up her CO from a hidden location in the stern.

The forward half of the *SunStar*—a spaceship built by the western alliance, led by the US—had crash-landed at the back of Smith's scrapyard at the end of World War III. The stern half had broken off and crashed on top of an old mine, creating a new crevice. The stern of the spaceship had ended up smashed, a long way underground. Out of sight, out of contact.

CO Mateo had survived.

And so, apparently, had Evelyn, who was now in the hands of our enemy, being tortured.

One cat, a tabby with a white chest, glanced slant-eyed at me in the predawn light and chuffed before looking away. I heard a faint sound in the night, right where the cats were staring.

Seven and a half meters of warbot suit appeared, looming, blocking out the last of the night's stars, as Mateo stepped almost daintily over piles of old scrap. His suit looked and worked like a huge spider—his three, five-and-a-half-meter-long legs telescoping and folding down until the matte-black torso and head of the suit were on a level with mine. A warbot could fit into much smaller spaces than it might first appear. He could fit through the back airlock to the office if he didn't mind getting his pretty chitosan paint job scratched. Mateo's scarred and misshapen human visage was visible behind a meter of horizontal silk-plaz view screen, vaguely like a single massive spider eye.

"Talk to me," he said.

"We've speculated that Warhammer captured and enthralled Raymond."

"Possibility acknowledged. Continue."

"I got a message today. I figure it means that Clarisse is coming for the goodies buried in the scrapyard."

The warbot didn't react. Mateo's hairless, scarred, misshaped head didn't move, but the scars around his mouth pulled, as if he knew the next bit would be bad. "You're not finished. Report," he snapped out, sounding like the Commanding Officer he had once been.

Gently, I said, "Evelyn's finger came in the mail. It was removed from her living body four days ago. No note. No return address."

Mateo stared at me. A juvenile pride cat bounded to his carapace, found no traction, and slid down the silk-plaz viewport, legs and claws scrabbling for purchase, falling. Mateo grabbed him out of the air, placing him on the dirt. The cat shook off the fall, his body language saying he meant to do that. Gathering his dignity, he sauntered into the darkness.

Mateo still said nothing, and I wondered how much of the situation he was processing. My friend—I guess he was still my friend?—had fairly significant brain damage from a nanobot attack, but I'd been trading for new Berger chip plug-ins to fill his brain with info, and they were helping him heal and process things.

According to my timeline, Clarisse Warhammer had learned, through Evelyn, about the *SunStar* at some point in the last six months. That had led the queen to Smith's Junk and Scrap, to Harlan, to the mine crack, and to the stern of the *SunStar* half buried at the back of the junkyard. Because we weren't expecting an attack, we hadn't been prepared. Mateo and I—and our unwanted visitor at the time, Jagger—had mounted the best defense we could when she attacked. That best defense meant that Warhammer had a good idea that there was Bug-alien tech and weapons in the office. And now, clearly, she had figured out who I was.

Mateo stared at me, unblinking, his face like a brick wall, showing no emotion. The cats got bored, and all but one sauntered away. As dawn began to gray the sky, Mateo said, "She wants the part of *SunStar* Evelyn told her about. Warhammer won't be informing the Law or the MS Angels. She thinks you're human, and she doesn't know about me, because Evelyn thinks I'm dead. She thinks you're weak and stupid, and she's taunting you, hoping you'll run scared if she gives you a warning. She thinks the Bug-tech is something we got on the black market, something small and localized. She doesn't know your office is a high-tech Bug ship. She thinks you got lucky last time and can be defeated. This time she'll bring more weapons. More men. How fast can she transition humans and create a nest?"

"I agree. And I don't know. I never tried more than one at a time, and I needed a med-bay for that. She may transition them without a med-bay and hope for the best, which would give her a faster turnaround time." My two successes were Cupcake and Jagger. Neither one of whom I had wanted as a thrall. I still wasn't sure if Mateo was a success or a failure.

Overhead, the last of the night's stars winked out as my friend raised to his full height and loomed over me. He wasn't going to hurt me, but my body tensed anyway, ancient fight-or-flight instincts trying to kick in.

Mateo was as close to cyborg as it was possible for a human to be. He was more machine than man, now, but he still thought and grieved at human speeds. The parts of his face that still worked twisted in anguish; his jaw and mouth tightened. He focused on me in the dim light. "We need the Simba," he said at last.

A Simba was a huge heavy battle tank built at the end of the war. It had weapons that could take out precision targets at five kilometers using aerial targeting systems; had lasers and jamming devices to bring down remote aircraft; had rail guns, blasters that could take down a platoon of warbot-suited warriors; had all the bells and whistles of a combat professional's dreams. It could be AI-directed, remote robo-guided, or warbot-suit operated, and some were built for multiple manning methods. Mateo was a warbot suit manned with a living breathing human, the best option of them all. Rumor had it this Simba was also mounted with a city-killer. With it, we could take out Warhammer, even if she was in an underground bunker.

"Can you leave for Charleston now?" he asked.

"Eight sharp," I said, "if you already got the AI-uplink prepared and the weapons affixed to the diesel."

"Jolene's comm unit is ready to go," Mateo said. "The EntNu uplink will go directly through to her."

Jolene had started out as a standard AI on the USSS *SunStar* half buried out back. Thanks to contamination by my nanobots, she had gained sentience and self-determination. She was now a Southern belle with attitude.

"Weapons mounted on the truck two days ago," he continued. "Its scanners are crap compared to the office's or my own, but are operational and integrated with the auto-targeting firing of the Para Gen. Did maintenance on armor and windows, but to fire reliably you'll need to be outside, meaning you have offense or defense options, not a combo. I installed eight mini-cams to keep track of the flatbed's contents, the cab, and the undercarriage. AC's running, but it won't last. Your trade gear's loaded."

"I'll get our personal gear and meet you out front."

"Roger that." Mateo moved silently into the gray of near dawn.

Cupcake and I were going on a road trip to dig up and steal a Simba. For that to happen we had to beg, borrow, or steal an earthmover. And we couldn't let anyone know. Yeah. Secrets.

We had known this day was coming for a while, and Mateo and Cupcake had come up with two different plans to rescue the Simba. They were full of holes so big you could guide a spaceship through them.

My version covered the details and utilized Jagger, a made-man with the Outlaw Militia Warriors. He had survived the Battle of Mobile. Three Simbas had been involved in the salvation of Mobile. So he might even have experience remote-driving one of the behemoths, should Mateo be needed elsewhere, like fighting in his warbot suit. Jagger knew weapons, and the OMW had contacts with the military. I'd contact Jagger once I got to Charleston. And I would be very careful not to touch him. Very *bloody* careful.

To get the Simba, I might need the cats' cooperation, which I had yet to obtain, but thanks to Warhammer's visit, the two prides had discovered a delight in war games and a taste for human flesh. Unless I was very mistaken, Tuffs—the Guardian Cat—would get a lot of pressure to send a cat crew to war with us.

By 7:40 a.m., the last of the valuables were fully secured on the flatbed of the diesel truck. All that was left was the camouflage junk. Gyro-balanced on armored legs, Mateo's warbot stepped over piles of scrap, carrying a couple hundred kilos of low-grade steel and pitted aluminum in his three servo-powered arms.

Banging everything around like a kid with old pots and pans, he positioned and secured the cheap scrap over the good stuff I was taking to trade, which included some high-grade steel, several hundred pounds of copper, and several dozen sterling-silver trays.

Cupcake had found the sterling in the same storage shed where she discovered the silver utensils, the dinnerware, and a box of gold-and-gem jewelry that she said was the real deal. The blackened trays had been plastic-wrapped, stacked five trays deep and three meters tall, in a shed I had never inventoried, and she had offered them up to us this morning, when Mateo told her we were implementing our plan early. Finding the silver and jewelry meant that Cupcake had earned her water usage several times over. Instead of stealing, I could trade for a working backhoe or dozer to dig out the Simba, if I could find a shady owner who would keep his mouth shut. And maybe I could outright buy a portable WIMP antigravity grabber to power up the Simba.

Mateo had fastened and strapped the scrap in the

bottom of the ancient flatbed, lashing it all down with flex before he positioned the truck bed's armored walls. The banging had brought cats from everywhere; dozens perched, watching from every vantage point. Tuffs was with them. By her body language—turned away—she was not happy with me. Walking flat-footed so I didn't step on a random kitten, I gently shoved cats out of the way and tossed my satchels into the niche built into the truck bed. Cupcake did the same with her gear, then jumped over the short truck-bed wall and arranged our personal bags so they were easy to get to and wouldn't bounce out when we hit potholes. Though still tentative, in the last two hours Cupcake had revealed a different side of herself as she helped to load for the trip, offering suggestions for trade items and chattering to Mateo. She had crazy-mad organizational skills.

As the other two worked, I climbed in the cab and checked the weapons. Mateo had long ago armored the diesel and affixed supports for weapons that could be rotated down for use and back into hidden compartments as needed. Only a fool traveled without protection, because there would surely be trouble. It was better to be prepared for everything than wake up dead.

Roadblocks created by local redneck thieves were not unknown. Assaults and disappearances were common. If the biker gang calling itself the MS Angels was moving east and taking territory, as rumors indicated, they would eventually hit Charleston, and the MSA were known to cover all their bases—meaning every road in and out. On the truck and on my person I was carrying multiple weapons of different calibers and energy usages, up close and distance weapons, as well as scanning and diagnostic gear. That stuff took up a lot of room, and in the cab, close at hand, was the only place I wanted it.

Spy, the many-times-great-granddaughter of the junkyard cats' queen, wandered all over the cab as I worked, sticking her nose into everything, getting in my way, and generally being a cat-pest. She *mrooowed* repeatedly, and I finally said, "The Guardian Cat said you can't go with me, so take up your argument with her. I'm not the cat-queen."

Spy looked at me and twitched her tail in clear disagreement, but she bounded out of the cab and disappeared, dodging around Mateo's peg legs.

"Tuffs is not going to be happy you sicced Spy on her," Mateo said, a hint of laughter in his mech voice.

"Yeah, well, with power comes responsibility. Or something like that." My Berger chip inserted: *With power comes great responsibility. The quote was spoken by Peter Parker's Uncle Ben, in—*

I shut it off. My chip input system needed an update. Usually that required outpatient surgery, but any surgeon or nursing staff who worked on me would likely be infected by my mutated nanobots, and I wasn't willing to have another thrall stuck to me like duct tape.

Tuffs leaped into the cab and landed on my back, her claws digging in. I yelped, and she jumped to the dash.

"That hurt!" I pulled my shirt out and reached up my back. "I'm bleeding! And why are you mad at me? The decision to not let Spy go was yours, not mine."

Tuffs arched her back, tortoiseshell hair standing out as if she'd been electrocuted, and she bared her canines. *Sisssss*, she said, the word and her body language majorly pissed off, leaf-green eyes narrowed. I thought for a moment that she was going to jump me again, but she stuck her head out, as if to say we needed to touch heads to communicate.

"Nuh-uh. No way. I'm not getting near you. I'm *bleeding*," I enunciated. And then I realized what had just happened and how it affected the pecking order, in a way that would not benefit anyone. I didn't get mad often, but I felt a little blood boil at the back of my skull. I dropped my blood-specked shirt and faced the Guardian Cat. Softly, so her people wouldn't hear me, I said, "Listen very carefully. And think back to before I came. You had to hunt rats and toxic bats to stay alive. Most of your kits died before they reached maturity. Starvation was a predator that followed you everywhere. Your males were dangerous, and the females traveled in gangs, fighting in groups to keep the males in their places. You remember?"

Tuffs narrowed her eyes to slits but closed her mouth. Her back slowly relaxed from its attack-mode arch. Her hair settled. *Hhhhah mmm*, she said.

"Right. I provide food and water because I want to, not because I *have* to. This is *my* junkyard. You do not get to chastise me. You do not get to punish me. If you try that again, I'll never defrost another body for your cats. You do not have opposable thumbs. You cannot do it without me."

Tuffs eyes went wide again, and her ears went flat. There were still a number of Clarisse's henchmen and women stored in the *SunStar*'s freezer, valuable protein for the cats. *Orrrowmerow*, she said, the sound that meant "this is a bad problem."

"Yeah. Bad," I said. I watched as thoughts flittered through her little cat brain. "So, how do you want to play this?"

Tuffs pulled her paws in under her, curling her tail against her feet. The tip twitched in agitation, but she was calmer. "*Meep?*" she asked, saying she was listening and wanted my attention too.

I tilted my head, catlike. "You scratch me again and there will be consequences."

"*Hhhhah mmm*," she said, agreeing, suddenly acting like a docile housecat.

Gingerly, one arm prepared for defense, I scooted forward in the passenger seat. I met her eyes and eased my head forward almost half the distance.

Tuffs sighed, her whiskers moving. Smoothly, she eased forward and touched my forehead with hers.

In her mind, I saw her love for Spy, her hopes, expectations, needs. Tuffs was old for a feral cat. Spy was from her most favored bloodline, what I understood was *Cat of Ours*. It was like a title and a complicated concept all in one. The cat part meant sneaky / savvy / smart / fighter / ambush-hunter / tracker / warrior / feline / female / person. The thought "ours" was imbedded with a long series of relationship constraints and successful territory and military maneuvers and a lot of bloodline pride.

Spy was a cat-of-value. Spy was important to both prides. Tuffs sent a query. "*Understand Spy?*"

Tuffs thought Spy would be the next Guardian Cat.

"Oh," I said. "You think she can lead, communicate with cat-ESP, and pass along the nanobots. A true queen." I sent a thought-concept to her about Spy needing to explore the world. To prove herself before the prides as worthy, a warrior of valor.

Tuffs, her whiskers tickling my face, made a soft sound of defeat, "*Huuuhhhnnn.*"

She sent visions of me protecting Spy, keeping her safe—the visions mostly of my body accepting gunfire and blades as I covered her.

"Yes." I agreed. "I'll keep her safe, as much as I'm able. But she's yours. She won't sit still or stay safe to make us happy. You know that."

Tuffs chuffed in disgusted acceptance. She sent me a vision of a clowder of seven cats, counting Spy, all in the cab with us on the road.

"Yeah. Fine. I'll get more kibble."

Tuffs backed away until I could focus on her eyes.

I blew out a breath and realized I was sweating bullets, my clothes stuck to me, my new scratches stinging. Taking my life in my hands, I stroked down Tuffs's back. Tuffs stiffened, then dropped her belly to the overheated dash and lifted her snout in the air in pleasure.

Cupcake appeared at the passenger window, leaning in, her head nearly touching mine. On her shoulder was Spy, who looked at me, one eye blue, one eye green. "Odd eyed," in Tuffs's vernacular.

I heard a chuffing sound and saw Tuffs staring at her many-times great granddaughter. "*Hhhhah mmm,*"

Tuffs said. She sent us a vision of Spy on the dash, riding away.

Spy received the thought-vision, and if a cat could smile, Spy did, satisfied and a little mean, as if she had won a dominance fight.

Tuffs hissed, jerked away from me, and stared daggers at Spy. Her ears were flat, and her green eyes were vicious. She said, "*Mrow. Siss.*"

Spy ducked her head and crawled off Cupcake's shoulder, inside the cab. She placed a paw on my arm and sent me a vision. I nearly jerked away in surprise. Spy's vision was colder, sharper like pine needles, tinted with a hint of icy green light. *A pile of freshly killed rats.* She blinked her odd eyes at me. I glanced at Tuffs, who was watching the exchange, quivering with emotion.

Spy stepped up and leaned in, our foreheads touching. The world skittered sideways as a memory slid into my mind, glass sharp. Intense. I wanted to hurl. *A toxic rat. A hunting cat stalking it. The bloody fight.*

"You want to hunt?" I asked her. "Waterfront rats are huge. You'll need to hunt in groups." I tried sending her a vision of hunting parties fighting with a single huge rat. Teeth like razors. Claws.

Spy hissed with excitement and hunched her shoulders, her whiskers grazing my face, her odd eyes staring at me. She whirled and leaped out the window. I hoped the communication we had just shared would allow me to talk to Spy without touch, the way Tuffs and I did.

In the truck bed, I heard Mateo shake the cargo, looking for scrap that might shift. Nothing substantial moved. Cupcake brought more dirt for cat litter and more kibble.

I finished securing the weapons, adding water and snacks. One-armed, I swung out of the cab and into the bed, where I checked Mateo's work, as he bent and checked my work in the cab. It was already hot, the temps at thirty-two degrees Celsius. I stank.

Mateo's warbot suit was air-conditioned. Not that I'd want to change places with him.

Once we were satisfied, I made a last stop at the office to use the body wand, change clothes, toss my toiletries into their small satchel, gather the laundry, and grab 2-Gen sunglasses to hide my weird orange irises. I hadn't been born this way. When I was transitioned the second time, by mech-nanos from a PRC Mama-Bot, the eyes were the result. To the bag I added a tube of orange lip gloss and a wide-brimmed hat that had belonged to Little Mama. For an Old Lady, my mother had been a fashionista.

I inserted the earbuds for the brand new long-distance EntNu comms system. In a worst-case scenario, where we survived an attack and needed a rescue, and where I was willing to risk the scrapyard, we could call for warbot reinforcement.

"Comms check?" I asked.

"Check," Mateo said.

"Check," Cupcake said.

"Check," said Gomez, the office's AI.

"Check, *Sweet Thang*," Jolene said.

I shook my head at Jolene's endearment. It was totally out of character for a spaceship-worthy AI, but she had chosen the name, the accent, and the Southern personality based on an old song. I wasn't going to quibble about her life choices.

"Okay," I said. "Cooler with food and extra water is in the truck's sleeping compartment with the stash of jewelry, extra ammo, cat litter, cat bowls, and the portable composting toilet. The bed is folded up out of the way to keep the cats off it."

"This place is going to reek," Cupcake said. She slid her eyes sideways to the cats sitting on the hood, watching. "No offense or anything."

She had a point. The cab would stink. Tuffs's reconnaissance clowder was Spy plus six cats: one solid gray, two gray tabbies, one orange tabby, one tortoiseshell, one pure black. Seven cats on a trip. At least two of the cats were intact males. Which reminded me to pick up med-bay supplies. Tuffs brought me several dozen cats every few months to neuter, and that used up supplies fast. It was a loss I accepted since it was far more humane than her previous method of claws and teeth that left the young males dragging themselves off to live or die. I stared at Spy. "No spraying. No marking territory. No using anything or anyone in the cab as a scratching post. Any cat who disobeys rides with the gear."

Spy made a little chuffing sound and looked at her squad. I had a feeling she was sharing the warning. Cats with ESP. *Bloody hell*.

Mateo's suit whirred at an almost inaudible level, and one of his shorter limbs came forward. Grasped in three of his fingers was a small black electronics box about ten-by-five-by-two centimeters. There were male and female ports on both sides with cords hanging from each. It looked like an amalgam of *SunStar* tech and old-fashioned tech, and I had never seen anything like it.

"This is an AI Interface Portal—the uplink for the Simba," he said. "When you dig down to a hatch, you'll see a port on the outside. Insert whichever end fits. The hatch will open. Remove the port and drop inside. You'll see a keypad, a schematic for a handprint, and a slot that looks like this." On Mateo's limb, a screen appeared, and it showed a tiny port, like a computer port from the mid-twenty-first century. "You'll have to manually hardwire the interface portal to the Simba by inserting this line into the slot. Input my command codes for the *SunStar*, verbally and manually, along with your handprint."

"Handprint? What about—?"

"You'll have to decontam. I've overwritten my handprint for yours in the IP. Jolene will do everything else and take over the Simba. Then you can activate the Grabber to power the WIMP engines, and I can drive it home."

"Really," I breathed. This little thingy, if it worked, would make my job much easier. "How did you figure it out?"

"I figured it out, darlin'," Jolene said over the earbuds. "And I created it in my very own lab. It's built according to the Simba specs in my memory banks."

I cupped my gloved hands and accepted the device, which was way heavier than it looked. "It's EntNu-based, isn't it?" I asked softly. Civilian Entangled Dark Neutrino tech had been taken away or disabled by the alien Bugs, along with the military's spaceships, at the end of the war. Now, EntNu-based devices were illegal for civilians. The *SunStar*'s military weapons were illegal for anyone. I could keep such devices safely in the scrapyard because they were well hidden by the *SunStar*'s background shielding. But if the military discovered this interface portal or the comms system, maybe at an official roadblock while I traveled, Cupcake and I would die in a Class Five Disciplinary Barracks.

"Yes," Mateo said. "But like the comms system on the truck, Jolene made certain it looks like prewar civilian hardware. I will be monitoring everything. You will not be *alone*, Shining," he said, his voice sounding almost human.

He knew. Mateo, more than anyone else alive, knew that I was always alone. Or I used to be. Now I had him and Cupcake. And the cats. And Jagger. I squared my shoulders. "What else?" When no one said anything, I slapped the side of the diesel and said to Mateo, Jolene, and Gomez, "You three have fun."

The clowder of cats bounded into the truck cab.

Cupcake, who continued to surprise me with her skill sets, climbed into the driver's seat and slid the nine-millimeter once carried by her husband into a wall mount that hadn't been there last time I checked. "I got this," she said and started the big engine.

"Oh. Well. Good then." I hated driving the diesel. My Berger chip wasn't programmed for the gears, and it was always hit or miss for me. I shoved the IP uplink onto the floor of the cab and against the front wall. The uplink instantly changed color to match the filth and for all intents and purposes, it disappeared. I grinned up at Mateo. "It's got Chameleon skin!"

"Of course. Did you think I'd put you in danger?"

"I think you want the Simba and keeping me safe is the best way to accomplish that," I said, sounding sour.

Mateo chuckled, a noise like rusty crowbars grinding together. I settled in to ride shotgun. Literally. A cat sprang to the dash. Spy. In charge.

Cupcake pulled out of Smith's Junk and Scrap, bouncing onto the old mining road. In the side mirror I watched as Mateo reset the alarms, the tire and track shredders, and other auto-defense measures. The rest of the cats were sitting in lines on the driveway, watching the warriors set off on an adventure. Or maybe it was a cat funeral, in case the travelers didn't make it back.

The old maps said Charleston, West Virginia was only sixty-seven miles from Smith's, but the condition of the roads (bad) and the condition of the bridges (worse) always made it a perilous three- to five-hour drive on roads infested with bandits and unprotected by lawmen on the take. I'd had to fight my way out before.

We made it to Naoma and turned up the rutted remains of West Virginia 3—Coal River Road, which followed the Big Coal River. Not so big since the damage to the atmosphere, but also not so well contained. Over the years, seasonal floods had washed out the asphalt in places, and the state had never repaired it; trees and bushes had intruded, narrowing the old road. It was slow going, but the big tires and the powerful engine pulled us through gullies, across small creeks, and over piles of brush.

As we crossed one particularly harrowing section of washed-out road, Cupcake asked, "Is it gonna be this way the whole trip? I can drive this rig through most anything, but this is nuts."

"Once we reach I-64 the road surface will be fine, because the state keeps the main transport system in good repair," I replied. "But, yeah, there's a lot of bad road and postwar crazy country in between."

She shrugged and steered the big truck into the brush to allow another vehicle to pass us. The road opened up after the next curve, and she worked through the gears, getting us up to speed, the windows down, cooler air blowing our hair, saving the air conditioning for later in the day. Cupcake started to sing, bellowing out an old R&B song, the melody, key, and beat, all questionable. Cupcake couldn't sing worth a lick, but she got high points for enthusiasm and volume.

We made it through what was left of Sundial, Stickney, and Montcoal without mishap, but just outside of Sylvester we rounded a bend to see a massive dead tree across the road. Three armed men on the other side. A car in the brush.

Cupcake reacted, too fast to be human. Slammed hard on the brakes. Opened the exhaust valves at the top of the compression stroke. The jake brake barked, like firing a gun. The flatbed started to slide, but she maneuvered it into a rocking stop in a cloud of dust and exhaust.

As the truck slid and bounced, Spy dove onto the dash, her mouth wide, showing her fangs through the windshield. She hissed at the armed men on the far side of the barricade, their weapons in full view. Two other cats joined her, leaning into the silk-plaz, quivering.

Dust billowed around us and into the cab.

I took in everything.

Three more men stepped from the brush, five yards away. Shotguns positioned, ready to fire. Not the Law. No uniforms. Dirty, sweat-stained clothes. Ancient sneakers or boots. Six against two. This looked bad.

The silk-plaz windows were down. We needed them up. But we needed to be able to fire. Mateo had said we have defense or offense. Not both. *Bloody hell.*

Cupcake said, "Let me handle this one."

"Go for it." I slapped open the overhead panel, and the refurbished M249 Para Gen II Belt-Fed, AI Integrated Machine Gun rotated up from below the window and into place.

Cupcake rolled her eyes. An honest-to-God eye roll. I hadn't seen one of those since before the war started. "Good God. You never heard of the delicate art of negotiation?" she asked.

"I've heard of it. I never saw it work against armed men." There wasn't time for me to put on protective equipment. This was going to hurt if I had to fire. I set the auto-target for the man in the middle. He froze as the targeting sights lit him up like a Christmas tree.

I jutted my chin toward the brush where the car was parked. Tied to a tree were two crying women who looked the worse for wear.

"That's what we're facing."

Cupcake looked at the women and back at the men. She gave a cat-worthy snarl. "Over my dead body." She leaned out the window. "Hey. Move the frickin' downed tree or my partner will shoot you boys to hell and back!"

They repositioned their weapons, ready to fire.

Cupcake leaned back in and said, "What're you waiting for? Fire that damn thing."

I fired.

The man in the center died instantly, a splash of red across the asphalt. Moving faster than anything human, I swiped off the auto-target. Swung the big gun right. Took out two more men. Hot brass bounced and scorched my bare skin. My eyes burned from nitrocellulose and gunpowder.

Cupcake leaned out. Fired three times. A fourth man fell. The two others vanished into the brush.

The cats on the dash soared out the windows. The rest of the cats followed, yellow, gray, and black smears of speed.

Cupcake said something, her mouth moving, any

sound lost beneath the concussive barrage. Opening her door, she jumped out. I deduced she had said, "Cover me." Cupcake landed as light as one of the cats.

"Roger that." I slid through and sat on the window ledge, engaging the sensors, swinging the Para Gen slowly from side to side. Watching for anything that moved.

Cupcake carried her weapon low, a two-hand grip, near her thigh. She crab-walked fast to the protection of the car. Cleared it. Cleared the far side of the rusted vehicle. Behind the car, she studied the underbrush. I had never asked, but it seemed Cupcake had weapons training. Or she had Berger-chipped the info and training, which meant she had some understanding and skill sets, but no muscle memory and no experience. I was going with the Berger.

Spy tried to get my attention. It was an intense spiraling sensation, part vertigo, part layers of green. Spy was in a tree, looking down on two men. The men who had run when Cupcake and I killed their pals. They were talking on old-fashioned walkie-talkies. The talkies had a limited but unknown range. My Berger implant supplied: *The range of coverage for long-range walkie-talkies increases with power. A two-watt radio can cover fourteen kilometers. A four-watt radio can reach up to forty-eight kilometers. All on flat terrain.*

Spy heard when the man spoke, and oddly, I heard too. "ETA twenty." Then, "Copy that. We'll be ready."

They had backup coming.

"Area is clear," I shouted to Cupcake, not caring if the men heard. "We have twenty minutes before reinforcements arrive."

Cupcake looked at me like I was nuts, scowled, and her face cleared, her mouth moving. "The cats. Right."

Through the earbud I barely heard Mateo, back at the junkyard, say, "Get off me you damn cats."

Cupcake placed her weapon on the hood of the car and pulled a knife I hadn't noticed. Deftly she cut the women free. They were Caucasian, a little older than me, and they were babbling. From body language and hand gestures, I deduced that they had been stopped and their bodyguard killed. They had been robbed and were about to be raped when our diesel approached. They babbled while Cupcake raided the dead men's pockets and found their keys, some cash, and several flasks of what was probably homemade hooch. She gave each woman a handgun taken from the dead men, ammo, and half of the cash, before helping them load their guard's body into the back seat of their car. The women took off, the fifty-year-old Ford spitting black exhaust. Even over my deafness, which would take several minutes to go away completely, it sounded as if it had consumption. It dog-tracked down the road on slick tires, but it was still running.

I checked my weapon, popped my ears, and draped ear protectors and goggles around my neck. My arms were pocked with faint burn marks to go along with the claw marks on my back. Sweat burned all of them.

Crawling into the sleeping compartment, I opened the box of ammo marked *5.56-by-45 millimeters*. On top of the packed rounds were ammo belts. I pulled out my replacements—one pre-loaded hundred-round ammo belt and two twenty-round belts—and made my way back up front. Removing my nearly empty belt (I had seven rounds left in it), I loaded one new belt and hooked the other belts into the secure loops on the passenger side floor. One hundred forty-seven rounds. That should do it.

"What's the plan? We gonna wait for them and take them down?" Cupcake shouted to me as she tried to drag a body out of the way. "I don't see a chainsaw. The rig isn't getting over that tree without some serious damage to the undercarriage."

"Can the diesel push it out of the way?"

She studied the tree and where it hit on the cab's grill. "I can try, but if it gets stuck, we're screwed."

"Try. Slowly."

"I don't like it. But I'll do it. The bodies?"

"Leave 'em."

"That's gonna squish." But Cupcake got back in the cab.

With a steady hand on the Para Gen and a firm grip on the truck's safety handle, I retook my place, sitting in the open window. I secured the weapon before I returned my attention to Spy. She was moving fast, and the contact was iffy. Without being head-to-head, I didn't know if it would work, but I sent her a picture vision of her hunting for the reinforcements and from which direction they would come. I got a hint of something dizzying which might have been Spy replying. Or not.

Then I lost contact.

Cupcake shifted into the lowest gear, a basso thrum that vibrated through my butt. The truck eased forward, and the bottom edge of the bumper connected, catching against the upper curve of the downed tree as she bumped it forward. It shifted but didn't roll. She reversed, stopped, and bumped it forward again. The tree, a long-dead native fir, shifted and rolled an inch. Cupcake repeated the process, getting a feel for the speed and force needed. Brittle branches snapped and broke, the dead tree moving in time with the truck bumps. The tree's own tapering shape allowed her to adjust the angle and speed of the bump as the tree began to roll in an arc, away from the road. Cupcake was right. The truck squished the bodies still in the road. We were making progress, but it was taking too long.

Spy concentrated on a house on a low mountain ahead, and sent me an urgent, vertigo-inducing vision of an armored log-cabin mansion with what looked like at least one cannon poking from its walls. There were four trucks, six motorbikes, and what might have been a Gov. car parked out front. It was a nice, secure hidey-hole.

In an upper window a naked woman leaned into the glass, arms up and braced. Even with long-distance cat eyes I couldn't see her expression, but I had a feeling of devastation. Behind her, another woman danced, clinging to a pole. She also wore an expression of dread.

"I'll be back," I said to the women, although I knew they couldn't hear me. "I'll get you free."

"What?" Cupcake shouted.

"Nothing," I shouted back. "A battle for another day."

From a garage-type door at the side of the house rolled two mini armored tanks, men riding on the outside. The mini-tanks careened down the hill toward Spy. There were weapons mounted on the mini-tanks, big weapons. I tried to focus in—

The vertigo worsened. The contact with Spy abruptly stopped.

I needed more guns. I dropped from the window and wiggled into the sleeping compartment. "Hurry," I said to Cupcake. "I think twenty minutes was a lot too generous." I brought a second weapon up. Beside the Para Gen, I attached a blaster—an Army Radiation-generated Active Denial Rifle II—the initials pronounced as *radar* among weapons geeks. The RADR fired a beam of radiation. It heated the fluid beneath a person's skin like a microwave, boiling the blood and cooking the internal organs. This model was lethal at anything under six meters. Between six and fifteen meters it created severe second-degree burns, blistering flesh. It was useless beyond that, giving the target a painful sunburn at most.

It didn't bode well for this trip that I was already breaking out the big guns and heavy ammo. In the past, they had been used only for show. All I'd had to do was display the weapons and we were allowed to pass. Something had changed.

It also didn't bode well that in order to fire reliably, I had to keep the passenger window down. I'd have no protection. I should have been wearing armor, no matter how hot it was today. Bad planning. Bad intel. Intel I used to get from Harlan. Dead Harlan.

I sent out a vision of Spy and her clowder returning to the cab at full speed. Hoped she got the word, or she and her cats would be left behind and would have to get home on their own.

Cupcake bumped, bumped, bumped, and the tree rolled forward, gaining momentum. I prepped the Para Gen and the RADR blaster to fire. Minutes passed as I added to my weapons stash, securing everything to the floor at my feet, rigs with holstered handguns strapped to my legs. As prepared as I could be, I braced myself for firing, sitting in the window.

"As soon as the cats get back, raise your window," I said to Cupcake. "We need the armor more than we need fresh air."

"It's gonna be hotter than homemade sin in here," she grumbled over the diesel.

Into my earbud, Mateo said, "The Para Gen will get hot, and it goes through ammo like a mofo, but it won't jam. To save ammo, I recommend you use autotarget and the AI."

I realized he was still in communication with the headsets and the cameras inside the cab. "Roger that. Setting for autotarget, three burst, manual fire. If I have to go fully auto," I said, "it'll be because I'm backed into a corner and have no choice."

Through the open windows, the cats dove and landed, claws out for purchase, digging into leather seats and our tender flesh.

Cupcake yelped and swatted a juvenile male who scored a bleeding scratch on her shoulder. Even enhanced by nanobots, she missed by a mile. Spy was the last cat in, and she skidded into place on the dash, claws ripping the old plastic. Her sides were working like a bellows, and she gave what sounded like an urgent *Mroooorow* of command.

Without pausing the bump, brake, bump, brake moving the fir tree, Cupcake raised her silk-plaz armored window and handed me her nine-millimeter. I removed the clip, inserting a full one and snapping it home with the heel of my hand. One handed, she slid it securely into the side pocket where she could draw it left-handed, if everything went to hell and back, I died, and she had to lower her protective window and defend herself.

I checked the chrono. Twelve minutes, twenty-eight seconds gone. My butt on the windowsill, I hooked a leg around my seatbelt, braced my thighs, and checked the Para Gen again. Another yard, and Cupcake began to swing the wheel, shoving the tree at a sharper angle. The tree bumped over the last dead body. The truck followed, the diesel rumbling, vibrating, and bouncing.

I pulled the ear protectors and goggles on. Loosened up my right arm. Stretched my fingers. Rolled my shoulders. Spy hissed a waring, her back arching, claws extruding and digging in. Hands flying, I checked the scanners.

Two tracked mini-tanks careened around the bend a half mile down the road. They spread out, moving at speed to block the road.

Cupcake cussed with great skill and originality over comms. She increased the speed of the bumping. The tree was rolling steadily.

Men jumped off the tanks and took cover. The scanners told me there were ten enemy combatants, but probably missed some. Counting the yahoos in the woods, that meant at least twelve targets, all armed.

The sensors were digesting info about the armaments we faced. Into my comms the scanners ID'd Spaatz, robo-capable mini-tanks. The tank on the right was mounted with a High Energy Weapons System—lasers. The scanner's AI recommended the laser as the primary objective, a five-millimeter diameter target that was bouncing all over the place. Faster than human, I merged the Para Gen to the sensors. The AI secured the tiny objective at the tank's upward bounce. Waiting.

I engaged auto-fire. It calculated range, speed and bounce of weapon and target, weather, wind speed—factors that I couldn't calculate. When the target bounced, the ParaGen fired a three-burst.

Shrapnel flew.

The attackers hadn't activated defensive measures. The men close to the road disappeared into the trees.

I slid the integrated AI back to manual fire, auto-targeted the tank on the left. Fired two rounds at what scanned as a rocket launcher on top. When that got me nothing, I fired a three-burst at the weapon's mounting system and targeting system. Shrapnel went flying.

"Bingo," I whispered.

The side-mounted weapons systems scanned as explosive-fired projectile launchers. Big-assed guns or small cannons. I fired. Hot brass landed on my arm and bounced off my face. The heat from the Para Gen scalded. I paused. Fired. Paused. Fired. Short bursts. All AI-assisted.

I finished the rest of the twenty rounds on the continuous tracks the tanks raced on, hoping to damage them enough to seize. One tank stopped, the other one turned as if a track was damaged, which meant the track systems had been replaced with aftermarket stuff, not military quality. I knew my junk. They had good weapons but hadn't spent the big bucks on vehicle support and transport. That was good news.

I changed out for the other twenty-round belt and spent it on targets in the woods. The Para Gen never jammed. Now I knew why Mateo loved this gun. It was dependable. And with the autotarget AI, it was bloody accurate. But. I had only the hundred round belt left after less than ninety seconds. Still lots of people to kill.

Bloody hell.

The truck's armor was taking small-arms fire. Cupcake slid low in the seat to make a smaller target, still bumping the tree. I was still hanging outside and might as well have a bullseye on my chest.

I didn't know if the tanks were totally disabled or if there were more weapons on them that the old scanner had missed.

The tree bounced out of the way.

The left tank fired. Rocked back and swiveled hard. I had taken out the targeting system and the missile flew over the truck cab.

"Bloody goat-fucking damn!" Cupcake shouted.

Mateo said into my earbud, "There will be a remote operator for each tank. They will have already offloaded into the trees. Each will be holding two controllers for tank and weapons systems or one larger integrated controller."

"Behind the squarish rock on the left," Cupcake said over comms. "Maybe a hundred feet ahead."

I pinpointed the form on the scanner and reset the Para Gen to full AI auto-target assist, manual fire. I fired three rounds. A man in faded black camo reeled off to the side. A bloody smear marked the rock. The tank on the left careened off the road and took two men with it.

Cupcake accelerated.

More men bolted out of the woods. Firing everything they had.

The glass at Cupcake's face was armored, but silkplaz wouldn't stand up to one of the massive rounds on the remaining tank or stop the laser if they got it going. I hit the Para Gen to full auto AI and let it take over. It took out four men and targeted the tanks again in the seconds it took me to detach the Radiation Active Denial Rifle at my feet. Then the ParaGen was beeping for more ammo. I had seven rounds in a belt on the floor. The tanks were coming up fast. I scrunched down below the window and let my reflexes take over. Aimed the blaster. Squeezed the lever. It took a sustained three-second burst at six meters or less to totally disable an enemy. Three seconds was forever. The only good thing was that the victims had no idea they were dead until they fell over.

One down.

The cab was taking heavy fire. Rounds ricocheted inside.

I fired again, ticking off three seconds with each blast. The truck lurched and I got one man with only two seconds' worth, but I left him screaming, so it was long enough.

Cupcake accelerated again, shifting through the gears as smooth as bacon grease.

I aimed. Fired. Another down. Cupcake rammed the side of the right-hand tank. I bounced all over the dash and back into my seat. The cats were on the floor, claws hooked into the rubber. I targeted the energy cell of one tank, then the other. I had no idea what a blaster would do to an energy cell, but I figured the radiation wouldn't help.

And then we were past the tanks. Past the enemy. I didn't know if there would be more down the road, so I kept the window down and fed my original belt into the Para Gen. Seven rounds. That was all I had left. I was breathing hard, and sweat was pouring off me, burning into my wounds.

The truck bounced and jarred across the broken pavement. Tree branches overgrowing the street made a rat-a-tat-tat along the cab and truck, throwing shards of tree and leaves inside. I ducked in and out to avoid them.

Time and miles passed. No one came after us.

What seemed like forever later, I said over comms, "I think we're good."

"Roger that," Mateo said.

At my words, most of the cats left the floor for the sleeping compartment. Spy bounced to the dash, settled in a supple coil, and began to groom her feet.

I pulled off the ear protectors and the goggles. Looked at Cupcake.

She was driving with all she had, her hands white, death grips on the wheel and the shifter, feet working the pedals, shoulders held high, her head still ducked low. Her blonde hair had fallen in little spiral curls around her sweaty face. She was breathing with her mouth open, her eyes wide and unblinking. I sat back in my seat and raised my window. We rode for several more minutes as the heat built. No one else appeared. No one else tried to stop us. The river to the side was trickling, summer dry. I opened a water bottle and drained it.

I opened another and held it out to Cupcake.

She took the bottle in one hand. It was shaking. Tears burst out and raced down her face. She took her foot off the accelerator and downshifted, coasting while she drank, her eyes on the road. When the bottle was empty, she passed it back to me.

"Most people saw some action in the war," she stated, sounding weirdly calm and composed despite the tears. "You?"

My insides clenched. I had night terrors about the war that left me gasping, screaming, and sweating, tears and snot all over me. "I was twelve when it started. I saw some action." Understatement of the decade.

"I never did. We got the training and the Berger chip upgrades, but we never had to use it. Me and my Old Man were living and working in Kansas City when it fell to the bots. Most of the Angels took off and resettled in St. Louis. Then that chapter was conscripted by the MSA." She wiped her face, leaving behind a wet sheen of tears. "We survived. I learned how to fire a weapon because I had to, but I never shot anybody. Killed anybody. Until today."

I looked out the window. The town of Sylvester passed by in a blaze of red metal roofs, fortified houses, and abandoned, dilapidated buildings. Cupcake turned on the A/C and cool air blew in, drying our sweat.

Neither of us said much until we hit I-64. Then Cupcake began talking again. A lot. About everything. Nonstop. Part of me wanted to punch her. The other part was glad to have her back from that panicked, near-silent fugue state.

Until she started singing songs from the thirties. They were probably loud and raucous back then, but they had probably been on key. Any key. At all. *Bloody hell*. Cupcake sang when she was excited, grieving, and while she was working in the scrapyard. I had a bad feeling that Cupcake sang all the time.

The Kanawha River still flowed through Charleston, though greatly reduced from its glory. The Elk River was a greasy, dried-up trickle, thanks to an old upstream oil spill and the lack of rain. But there was enough water in the bigger river to create a green landscape—farms planted with corn, tobacco, and cotton, huge greenhouses producing tons of vegetables. There was a five-year-old water purification plant that allowed the local Gov. and its citizens to sell water from Charleston's negotiated water rights.

I didn't come here often. Besides the dangerous journey, the water and the greenery were too painful, reminding me of the cool, wet, green Washington State of my childhood. All lost.

Everything here was different. In the aftermath of a water-rights war, Charleston had developed a Wild West environment with water as the basis for its burgeoning wealth. In a world of violence, Charleston was less safe than most bigger cities to the east, but not as horrible as some places to the west. People, trade, and money—and the opportunity to *make* money— flowed through here. The Hand of the Law worked to keep peace so that money could flow.

Unknown to anyone but Mateo and me (I hoped), there was a Simba buried near the city. Whoever rescued the World War III era battle tank would have the power to take over Charleston and the water rights, and rule like a king. Until the military came after them. If that battle-tank owner was me, I might even be able to force a truce with the military and stay in charge, defeat the MS Angels, and make everything better. If ruling was what I wanted. Which it wasn't. Mostly I just wanted what Pops had wanted: to keep the weapons of war out of the hands of the PRC and local warmongers, which would keep the Earth out of the targeting sights of the Bugs. But Pops had built his plans without knowing what I would become when infected by bicolor ants and then swarmed by Mama-Bot nanobots. And he'd had no idea about queens and nest builders and what Clarisse Warhammer would become.

This was the thing about riding shotgun. Too much time to think. Too long listening to Cupcake caterwaul. Too much leftover headache from firing weapons and talking to Spy.

We arrived at the Courtyard Inn near the confluence of the Kanawha and Elk Rivers, where Cupcake parked the rig like a pro in the hotel's secure parking area. She was chattering about the trip she and her dad took across country when she was a kid and he was a long-haul trucker, nattering on about the wonders of St. Louis, when she turned off the big diesel. "That arch was amazing. Nothing like it in today's world. You shoulda seen it—"

"Cupcake, I have a headache."

"What?" She went pale, swiveling to me in the big leather seat. "What can I do? Can I get you some medicine? Aspirin?"

I pulled on my 2-Gen sunglasses and gave her a pair too. "Ice water. A fourth-floor room with a fully functional AC and its own bathroom with hot water would be nice. Why don't you check us in and I'll unload. And if they have an operating phone system, here's the appointments we need to make and supplies we could use." I slapped cash into her hand, and she bounded from the cab, happy to have a job to do. Blissful silence settled on me. Three cats pattered out of their sleeping quarters and jumped to the dash. Spy did cat yoga and yawned.

"Mateo?" I asked through my comms. He didn't answer. I was fairly certain that he had disconnected about the time Cupcake started singing. I gathered the weapons and stuffed them into their cases and boxes. Because that kept them from looking like guns. *Right. Sure it did.*

I was "sick," so Cupcake rushed back in a dither with the room key and slapped it into my hand.

"Fourth floor, just like you said. And they have elevators! They work, too, from 6:00 a.m. to 6:00 p.m. Shall I make arrangements for lunch?" She flipped open a small spiral notebook and studied her notes.

"Sure. Protein. Beef, rare but not bleeding. Potatoes if they have them. Anything green. And I'll pay good money for a nice cold beer. I'll secure our cargo and take up the suitcases, weapons, small valuables, and cash."

"Good by me. But you lay down, you hear?" She took off like a scalded dog.

I shook my head, pulled on my gloves so I didn't infect anyone, grabbed the gear, and headed to the elevators, the seven cats racing along the walls. No one saw us, and the cats were blissfully silent, diving inside as the elevator opened. That alone was odd enough to make me wonder if they were using their cat ESP to stay hidden.

Room 402 had two beds, a big bathroom, a pull-out sofa, and two chairs. I turned on the AC. It rattled and shook, smelling sour until it started cooling the room. *Bliss*. After using the flush toilet, I washed the gunshot residue off my skin in a short but warm shower—the time determined by the faucet's water regulator—inspected my wounds, smeared hotel moisturizer over me, and tried Mateo again. I cussed him thoroughly when he didn't answer.

I set out a sizeable litter box and a bowl of water for the cats, while they inspected the room, drinking out of the toilet—a water toilet, not a composting one—by choice, climbing atop the sofa to look out the window. Claiming beds and observation posts. Thankfully, they left me a small space on one mattress. Using the hotel's satellite communication, which would have no security at all, I formatted and sent a text message to my favorite OMW asshole—make that my only OMW asshole—then stretched out on the oh-so-comfortable bed, an arm over my head, and closed my eyes.

When Cupcake returned to the room, banging open the door, she woke me from a sound sleep. "Get up, sleepyhead," she said, "and take these aspirin. We have a lunch bar featuring steaks big enough to use as baseball mitts, scheduled *now*, with beer and wine. *Cold*. I checked. At Urgands, across the Elk. Then hot soaky baths, massages, and mani-pedis."

"No massage, no mani-pedi," I said, still hiding my face. I'd infect anyone who touched me skin to skin. That was how I ended up with Cupcake. Only queens could pass the nanobots that transitioned biological creatures into whatever we were, and Cupcake wasn't a queen. She could get massaged and get her nails done, no problem. I was dangerous. "But the hot bath sounds wonderful."

"But—"

"No buts," I said.

"This is just so stupid."

This being that I never allowed anyone to touch me.

I opened my eyes beneath the protection of my arm. That sounded like independence. Not at all like thralldom. I smiled slowly. "Yeah?"

"The nail techs wear gloves," she announced with something like glee.

"Really?" *Gloves*? I could have a mani-pedi?

"Really."

"You are hereby promoted to the woman in charge."

I could practically feel her delight on the air like glitter, rainbows, and choir music. "You'll take the massage, too?"

"No, but yes to the lunch, the beer, the bath, and the mani-pedi. And the aspirin." Cupcake rattled the pills like dice and dropped them into my hand. I knocked them back with the icy water she held out. It wasn't metallic and old, like the stored water I drank at the junkyard, but fresh and pure. Pure, prewar-style paradise. For this alone I envied Charleston. I closed my eyes, grieving for the world before war and a WIMP bomb—Weakly Interacting Massive Particle bomb—left this dried-out husk of a planet. "What else did you do?"

Cupcake said, "I arranged for the laundry to be picked up, cleaned, and delivered back to our room, and I told them to wear gloves like your note said. I hired an armed escort for the night, which, according to the concierge, will keep us from standing out as young and foreign among the locals. She got us reservations at 7:00 p.m. at a restaurant I heard about. I put a call through to Morrison's Foundry, Metals, and Scrap, that contact who purchased your high-grade metal in the past?" she reminded, as if I might have forgotten my own contacts and the info on the notes she had taken. "We'll see him in the morning at the foundry. He's offering us breakfast."

"That's . . ." I sat up slowly on the bed. "Cupcake, did you hold a rank in the Hell's Angels?"

"Yes. Well, as much as a woman can. And that changed a lot when the MS-13 took us over." Her face went through a series of emotions, too fast to follow, except they had all been bad. "Things changed after that," she said flatly.

Gently, I asked, "What did you do with the Angels?"

"I was the communication and records specialist for the president."

My eyebrows rose nearly to my hairline. That was an important job in any organization.

She tried for nonchalant, but I could see the pride beneath her words. "I handled all appointments, kept the calendar straight, and kept the contact info for every chapter, every Enforcer, and every made-man in Hell's Angels."

"I'm impressed."

Softer, she said, "Yeah. I used to be impressive as hell. When word came that the Mara Salvatrucha had gone to war with us and were trying to force a merger, I hid it all. They never got my contact info. I protected my people. But my Old Man changed after the takeover. Things were never the same between us."

She took a breath as if tucking old pain away, and slapped my thigh. "Let's go get that bath."

"Cupcake? Do you think the MS Angels, maybe Warhammer herself, were responsible for the attack on the road? They were using Spaatz mini-tanks, same tanks that attacked the junkyard."

"I hope to hell not, because that would mean she's already moving in or one of her people gained access to junkyard comms when they attacked you there."

How had that not occurred to me? I tapped my earbud. "Mateo? Are you there? What do you think?"

"Cutting transmissions. Rerunning our security software. Analyzing the IT capabilities of the log house." That meant using the *SunStar's* comms and a satellite. *Dangerous*.

The comms went silent again. We were on our own.

I slid down and rocked back my head on the porcelain rim, water up to my chin, silky bubbles all through. It smelled like gardenias, remembered from my youth. And it was hot, so hot the air steamed and water dripped down the white tile. So hot my blood wanted to turn to sludge and my skin was sending reports to my brain about blistering off my flesh. It was a fraction of a degree from actual damage. It was perfect. And because lots of water—especially hot water—killed my mutated nanos, I could empty the tub, wipe it down, and not infect anyone. I could relax. Totally relax. It was amazing.

Cupcake, on the other side of the short wall, was in her own tub, not talking. At last. The only sounds were her snores, the plink of water falling, the gurgle of the water heater in the next room, and . . . nothing else.

All the tension began to ease out of me. I was facing problems and peril and combat, but I had survived a battle with sex bandits outside Sylvester, had a belly full of beef, and my head was full of hoppy happiness from the four kinds of beer brewed at Urgands. Beef was a treat so expensive I could afford it only once or twice a year, and getting even a little soused was risky. But I had two cats patrolling outside with the human guard recommended by the hotel, and a SOG SEAL 2100 knife under the towels on the table beside the tub. I was reasonably safe. And clean. I closed my eyes and let sleep pull me under.

After the bath, I got my first professional mani-pedi by a woman wearing gloves, while Cupcake got a massage. My feet and hands looked fabulous, not that they would stay that way for long working at a junkyard. While Cupcake was treated to her mani-pedi, I got my hair professionally trimmed by the same woman who did hands and feet, and who agreed to wear gloves once I promised a hefty tip. After, she used this amazing goopy stuff that made my short hair spike up like bristles. I stared at my reflection, dressed in an orange top, a full swingy skirt (to hide my knife), with adorable little platform shoes, lipstick, Kajal (desert-dweller's heavy eyeliner), and my orange-lensed 2-Gen sunglasses to cover my funky eyes. With the thin lacy gloves, I looked fabulous.

Cupcake looked just as grand in my mother's pink silk skirt and peasant top, with pink Kajal and sandals. We indulged in another beer, fresh fruit—*bloody hell* I had missed strawberries—and we were done with being pampered. I paid the outrageous bill, and Cupcake and I walked into the afternoon. I nodded to the bodyguard and spotted Spy peeking around the corner from the nearby alley.

Everything looked fine, but the cat's shoulders were high, and she blinked at me, and I understood she was telling me that we were not completely safe. She looked across the street. An electric delivery truck slid past us along the roadway, nearly silent, blocking my view. When it passed, I spotted the man across the street.

Adrenaline spiked through me like cactus sliding along my nerves. My heart raced. His Harley was parked in the shade of a dusty tree, and he was braced, sitting sideways against his bike seat, facing me. This Harley was an older model with no defensive armament or visual shielding. No visible weapons on bike or rider.

His legs were stretched out, ankles crossed, arms folded across his massive chest. He was leaner, harder than only a few weeks past, his muscles defined beneath the thin, UV-blocking, long-sleeved T-shirt and dusty black jeans. He was wearing biking boots and the barely visible Morphon on one wrist, a metallic wristband on the other. Black anti-glare sunglasses. His hair was slightly longer than before. Rings on every finger like fancy knucks for fighting.

No weapons. And, most important, no OMW kutte. He was here, undercover, as I had requested in my message. Requested. Not ordered. And to be here so fast, he had been close by. Though I had left my own outdated Morphon turned off, he had found me, in a city of nearly a hundred thousand people.

The connection between us was electric, but I didn't reach for him. I curled my fingers under, fighting that urge that made me a queen in my species.

A hot breeze whirled down the street, my dress swishing around my legs.

Jagger puffed once on a cigar, the mellow scent and smoke curling along with the wind. He didn't move otherwise.

"Ohhh my. Girl, is that who I think it is?" Cupcake whispered.

"Yeah," I breathed. "Remember to call me Heather."

"Mmmm, Mmmm, Mmmm," she hummed, as if he were delicious.

Cupcake had been healing in the med-bay and then going through the transition—for the second time—in the days following Clarisse Warhammer's attack and defeat at the junkyard. But she and Jagger had been together for several critical days of their transitions. What did he remember? The memories I had implanted? The full truth? Or a warped combination of the two?

"Wait here," I said to Cupcake. I stepped off the curb and crossed the narrow street. From the corner of my eye, I saw Spy dart over. Then two more cats, dark streaks. My cat-guard clowder. The bodyguard followed behind me, and I could practically smell his biochemical markers flood with fight-or-flight pheromones. "He's okay," I murmured to the man, hoping I was right. "Wait with Cupcake." The guard stopped and backed up. He took Cupcake's arm and pulled her into a shadow.

I stepped into the shade of the tree, into Jagger's personal space, and stopped. He smelled of exhaust and sweat and cigar. He smelled of the past, of the same scents my father had carried, the scent of OMW and the open road.

"Jagger," I said softly.

Talking around the cigar clenched in his teeth, he said, "Heather. Or Shining. Which is it this time?" His voice was low and gravelly and vibrated through his chest, through the air between us, and into me. His question let me know that he remembered more than I wanted him to. Remembered enough to be dangerous to me and to the junkyard. And my nanobots wanted him, wanted to take him to my bed and—

No. That would be totally unfair to him. I had to feel my way through this meeting. "You came."

"Didn't have a choice, did I?"

I tilted my head at him, studying his body language, tone, the facial muscles visible below his dark glasses.

"What did you do to me?" he asked. "You and that Bug ship you call an office."

Fear sang through me. He remembered not just what had happened in the fight and during his healing time in the med-bay, Berger chips running. He had been able to figure out even more. We had never talked about the alien ship buried in the junkyard.

"I did nothing on purpose. You touched my stuff. You got infected. Who have you told about me? About the junkyard?"

"No one." He lifted a hand to the cigar, puffing several times to keep it alight before he removed it from his mouth, raised his glasses, and glowered at me. "Whatever you did to me, it kept me silent. I wasn't even able to text or email the info. Hell, I couldn't even whisper it to myself." He was furious, but that fury was leashed. So far. "I planned to come here today and gun you down in the street just so I could be free of you. But I couldn't pick up a weapon this morning. Not a handgun, not a blade. What. Did. You. Do. To. Me?"

Spy sent me a vision of Jagger and me as seen from above. She and her cats were in the tree. Her claws were out. She was staring at the spot on Jagger's unprotected neck where she would land and bite him.

I nearly reeled from the visual connection and broke it with an effort. "Nothing," I said again. "I have a disease. You caught it." *Infection. Disease.* Good words. They hid the truth in plain sight.

"I'm faster. I heal quicker. I see better than I did. And sometimes . . ."

I waited.

"Sometimes I think I smell you, hear your voice. I research stuff, track people. I've always tracked the MS Angels, but now I'm watching my own people in case someone's in contact with them. Without OMW orders. Just doing it because you might want me to. I have new contacts all over the scrap-business world, and when I should be sleeping, I plan how to buy scrap from you and how to send you weapons and tech. I came here today *without weapons*. Because I'm a damn fool, and all I could think about was you." This time he whispered, "What did you do to me? What is this *disease*?"

I could take him over again, as fully as the day he rode away from the scrapyard. It would be easy, a single touch, my bare palm to his. I could make him mine, a thrall, as servile as Cupcake had been. Or I could give him his freedom, as much as possible, and tell him the truth. That was a novel idea.

"You know the nanobots that were put into the *Cataglyphis bicolor* ants?"

Accessing his Berger chip for the info, he inclined his head slightly and said, "Using bio-nanos, military and Gov. created ants to scavenge dead flesh, to clean up the rotting corpses in the cities so they could be habitable again. The ants were supposed to die. Instead, a few of them—thirteen, they think—mutated. One became a female, creating a new, reproducible species. *Cataglyphis bicolor fabricius*. Instead of being solely scavengers, they became predators."

"They swarm and attack any human they find," I said.

"They're impossible to eradicate because they can change sexes and start a new nest. What does this have to do with what you did to me?"

"The queens can transfer the bio-nanobots to any human who survives being swarmed."

"*No one* survives swarming."

"Three of us did. A guy named Sherman Griffith. A woman named Catherine Warren, AKA Clarisse Warhammer of the MS Angels. And a twelve-year-old girl named Shining Smith, the daughter of the prez of the Outlaw Militia Warriors." I peeled down the wrist of my glove to expose the scars. They were rippled, ragged, bumpy, pitted, and still red. I returned the wrist cuff to position. "That survival makes the victim a carrier. Only survivors of a direct queen attack, so far as I've been able to find out, can transmit the nanobots by deliberate or accidental touch. Or by someone touching the things recently touched by us."

His body went taut, ever so slightly, and his jaw tightened as he put things together, things that had happened when he was inside the office of the junkyard, touching my things with his bare hands. To cover that minute reaction, he lifted the cigar. Puffed. I really wanted a cigar, suddenly. It had been years since I'd had one.

"So, I'm what? A slave?" His Alabama accent hard and rasping, he growled the last word. He stood. Too close.

"Not exactly. I call them thralls. You have free will, but you're bound by protective instincts and a desire to please me."

Jagger whipped out his hand and yanked me to him. My breasts were smashed against his chest, his hand a vise on my arm, bruising me. "Please you?" He dropped the cigar and gripped the back of my neck. "Let me show you how I want to please you."

His mouth landed on mine. Heat and need and want blasted through me, through the bare skin of his palm on my neck. His tongue invaded my mouth. He tasted of cigar and Jagger. And I knew in that moment he had been part of my dreams. All of my dreams. Jagger, top enforcer to the OMW, had been inside my dreams, my sex dreams. He knew what I wanted. How to please me. *He knew me.* And I knew *him*. And on some level, neither of us cared if we were more tightly bound as long as we could have this.

My arms went around his shoulders. His tongue plundered my mouth. His hands gripped my ass and he hauled me up against him. His need was hard and huge against my lower belly. I raised my legs, wrapped them around his waist.

Bloody damndamndamn. I *wanted* this man. His beard abraded my face. He tasted of sex and cigar and . . . beer. He tasted of *beer*. I swirled my tongue around his. Sucked it into my mouth. I moaned deep into him, feeling the vibration of need against my core.

"Hey, you two," Cupcake said, her voice intruding on . . . *this*. "You're attracting a crowd. Unless you want to put on a free sex show, you should stop *now*."

"Get a room," a strange voice shouted.

I pushed back from Jagger. "Stop," I whispered, gasping.

"No," he whispered back, one hand sliding around front and up under my skirt. Electric heat shot through me.

"Stop," I begged.

"I'll stop, but this ain't over, Little Girl. I'll have you or die trying."

I rested my arm across my eyes, trying to shut out the headache that was returning, driven by Cupcake's insistent voice. "Jagger is hot. He's like chocolate sex on a stick, melting in the summer heat. If he was any hotter, he'd melt the ground he was standing on. That man would do anything for you, girl. You got to stop being such a—"

"Stop." I did not want to hear what Cupcake thought of me. Life was too short for that kind of condemnation.

"I will not stop. We need that man for our nest."

I dropped my arm, turned my head, and looked at my thrall. Or . . . my not-thrall.

Cupcake was wearing pajamas, her blonde hair up in a sprout tail atop her head. Her face was set in a mulish expression. "We need him. We need him to find an earthmover and help get the Simba out of the mud. He survived the Battle of Mobile. The Simbas were the only weapons that survived the battle. Jagger survived, ergo he was in a Simba, so he probably knows how to drive one."

"Ergo?" I asked, my mind on her deeper meanings, things I had thought myself.

"It's a good word. Ask your Berger if you got no education," she said, sounding a little mean.

"I know what it means. And yes, we do need him." I needed and wanted him in the worst ways possible. But not while sharing a room with Cupcake and the cats. No. Never. "Before he left the scrapyard, I put him to work," I said, knowing the headache wasn't going to be babied. "Just a few suggestions, things he might want to do. They took, even if getting away from me decreased their effectiveness. He's halfway to becoming my new Harlan."

"He'd make a good Harlan. He'd make a better nest-mate."

I had planted memories of a meeting and discussion in Jagger's brain, though the person I intended him to remember was my fake boss, a burly macho man, not the girly accountant named Heather. I'd given Harlan's contact list to Jagger and told him there was a traitor to the OMW in it. That person likely had access to contacts in the Gov. and was making alliances with the MS Angels. Jagger had said it had to be a cell of people, not just one. Before he rode away, he'd said he'd be breaking bones and busting teeth to find the traitors. That was an enforcer's job. But I hadn't intended my suggestions to steal his sleep and make him less effective. Or to make him think about me twenty-four seven. Or link our sex dreams.

"I'm right. You know it." Cupcake said.

I closed my eyes and didn't respond to her comments, saying instead, "I'll have to go after the MS Angels' leadership eventually, as soon as Jagger gets intel on the traitor cell in the Gov. and in the OMW. But first we rescue the Simba. Then we rescue Evelyn and kill Clarisse."

I didn't add, *and in between, rescue women in the log cabin in the hills*. Cupcake hadn't seen the women, and she had bad memories she had never shared. No need to stimulate them. But . . . Yeah. I was going on a rescue mission of my own.

A Simba would come in handy for that. Someone in the Gov. had made an alliance with the bloody bedamned MS Angels. And one cell of Angels was led by a queen, like me. Every time I thought about that I got cold chills. When Cupcake started to reply I said, "I have a headache. Wake me in half an hour. Then we'll go for supper."

"We should ask Jagger."

"We're not asking Jagger. We're doing girl's night out, remember?"

"He's hot. I'll take him if you don't want him. But I saw how you kissed Mr. Sex on a Stick. You *want* him."

"Half an hour," I sighed and let myself ease into sleep.

We had reservations for Italian, or as Italian as anyone could get these days, at Marconi's Famiglia, a famous addition to Charleston's restaurant offerings, run by old man Marconi, his four sons, and three daughters. The restaurant had dim lighting, starched white tablecloths, cloth napkins, fancy plates and utensils. The waiters wore black pants and white shirts with red-checked aprons. Soft music played in the background. Wine bottles were everywhere. Old wood floors gleamed. Candles flickered. *Yes*. Prewar ambiance. It all set the mood for fabulous food. And a wine list that was outrageously *expensive*.

I ordered chicken Marsala with real made-from-wheat-and-not-potato-flour pasta and a lettuce salad big enough to choke on, and a beer. Cupcake started out asking for the same thing but changed her mind when I said she could get what she wanted. She ordered a Caprese salad, bruschetta, and chicken Carbonara with pasta. And a big bottle of wine.

I had now officially busted my entire personal budget for the year. A frisson of fear swept through me, followed by relief when I remembered again the sterling silver Cupcake had found in the scrapyard. I could buy all the ammo I needed and still afford a night out. I could call it employee bonuses and the Gov. might let me slide. I looked around Marconi's with a less jaundiced eye. A girl could do worse for a business expense.

For the fourth time, Cupcake asked, "Do I look okay?" She smoothed her dress down her thighs. "I never wore dresses when I was riding. Me and my old man, we rode with just a backpack between us." She held out a foot, admiring her new, sparkly shoes. They were prewar, new in the box, scavenged from somewhere, and only a little too tight. "Do I look okay? Does it make me look fat?" She stroked the dress again.

"No. Cupcake, you look . . . radiant," I said, trying for a new word that would satisfy her more than *pretty*, *beautiful*, and *fancy* had. "That dress makes you look like a princess. All the sequins, the pearls, and the gauzy . . ." My hand flapped in the air, waiting for the Berger chip to help me think of a word. It didn't. ". . . dress parts. And I like your hair curled like that." It was loose, a curly bouncy blonde that swayed when she turned her head. "Marconi's sons are practically drooling over you."

"Not me. You. You look beautiful," she gushed.

Unlike Cupcake, I had worn dresses all the time, up until the start of the war, when my mother died riding bitch seat behind Pops, shooting at the invading PRC. I had outgrown all my own dresses, but Little Mama's clothes fit perfectly, and our coloration was similar enough that I could wear her entire wardrobe. My mixed-race heritage gave me golden brown skin that looked like a very, *very* dark tan, and my hair was dark with sun-bronzed streaks.

At Cupcake's insistence, I was wearing one of Little Mama's cocktail dresses in a lustrous black that picked up a dark, old-gold sheen in the right light. The skirt was loose enough that I wore a wicked six-inch blade strapped to my left thigh and a small-cal semiautomatic on the right. And because Little Mama had been no fool, the dress had bottomless pockets on both sides so I could retrieve both weapons easily. I was also wearing a pair of Little Mama's fancy earrings and a necklace. And lace gloves to protect anyone from being transitioned accidentally by my touch. The ensemble looked a little odd with the pale-blue sunglasses, but I hadn't known what the lighting would be like in Marconi's. It was dim enough that I put the glasses in my tiny bag, which I placed on the floor beside my strappy black heels. I'd be in trouble if I had to run, but with our bodyguard, that was unlikely.

The big bearded fellow was waiting outside with the other bodyguards, and the cats, who were patrolling the neighborhood. I could feel them in the distance, like a faint itch in my brain, though that made no sense at all. They were having a wonderful time, chasing big roaches and house mice and shadowing humans they thought were suspicious. Which was so cute.

The salads came, along with the bottle of wine, a Marconi son going through the entire cork-sniffing routine, even though the cork was plastic. It was a Carolina red, sold in black bottles to look as if they had been burned in a fire and rescued. Which sounded gross, but whatever. I didn't drink much wine.

The waiter poured wine into Cupcake's stemmed glass and placed a beer in a cut-crystal stein at my elbow before departing. If he leered at us a little, I let it go. We *were* pretty cute.

"Thank you. It's been ages since I had wine." Cupcake held her glass up to me, and I clinked my stein to it. "To friends," she said, sipped, and made a little moan of delight.

Friends. That word knotted up inside me. It was a lot more personal than *thrall*. And I had never had a friend. Except Harlan and Mateo. Harlan was dead because of me, and technically Mateo was still a thrall.

Friends. I lowered my stein and sipped. It was good beer. It tasted of . . . friendship.

For some stupid reason tears burned my eyes. I blinked them away.

I knew nothing about small talk, but for Cupcake and her dreams about being a high-class lady on a girls' night out, I'd try. "Tell me about the gorgeous shoes and that dress. Where did you find them?"

She made a little squeak of pleasure and launched into the details of her shopping spree, which had taken place while I napped. I listened with half an ear, keeping an eye on the restaurant patrons, the Marconis, and catching sight of a cat on the outside windowsill, looking in. Staring at me.

The world spun and vertigo hit me with a green-and-silver vision of motorcycles with black and blue and green-flame paint jobs. Spy blinked at me and dropped away. I tried to ask her, *What? What's with the bikes?* But she was gone. And I had no idea what she was showing me, except some really cool motorcycles. I didn't get the sense of danger or attack, just bikes.

My balance restored itself as Cupcake nattered on. And on. She told me details about every single store she had visited. About a lending library where she sat reading old magazines. About a movie theater showing the latest Ms. Robo-Marple thriller.

Everything seemed fine, though the cats disagreed with that assessment. I ate my salad. Drank my beer. And then the main course came.

The smallest Marconi son brought out a pretty folding stand and a big tray containing four plates— our order and two others. The dishes that weren't ours were a platter of triple-cheese-stuffed manicotti and another holding a small whole roasted chicken with fresh herbs (heavy on the rosemary) and sautéed green beans, enough to feed two starving adults. But instead of taking the extra food to another table, he arranged the plates at our table, poured a single glass of wine, and brought up one more chair. He left.

I looked at Cupcake. She went scarlet and made an honest-to-God titter.

"*Cupcake?*" I said, the word laden with suspicion.

"I. Well." She twirled a pale curl around her finger. "It just seemed . . . I mean, I thought . . . I ran into—Here he is!" She jumped to her feet and waved at the door. Where Jagger stood, wearing a black suit and a perfectly starched white shirt, open at the neck.

"*Bloo-dy damn*," I whispered.

Jagger, top enforcer to the vice president of the Outlaw Militia Warriors, had been bad-boy dangerous in riding gear. Gorgeous in black jeans. But standing in the inner door, wearing a black suit . . . he was devastating. A shiver shuddered through me.

Built like a brick shithouse: small waist, broad shoulders. *Oh. My.*

His brown hair was slicked to his skull, blacker in the dim light. His eyes were heated, his mouth in a dangerous scowl as he took in the restaurant and every person in it. He flexed his hands into fists, the rings on every finger moving like the disjointed knucks they were, glinting in the low light. He met my eyes, his containing a warning.

Liquid heat stroked through my middle and spread out as if someone had lit a flame inside me. My bio-mech nanos hadn't forgotten the kiss—*oh God, that kiss*. They wanted him almost as much as I did.

In that black suit, in the rarefied glow of Marconi's candlelight, he looked even bigger than before. Fast-looking and rangy, if rangy was also big enough to play offensive tackle in the NFL, except leaner now. Meaner.

Bugger.

Suddenly, a black cat raced in the door, whirled past Jagger, and sprang onto my table, his feet missing the platters, his feral green eyes like emeralds. He hissed at the kitchen, fangs bared. He hissed again, a much louder noise than his small body should be able to make. He was staring at the concierge, one of Marconi's sons. The man was racing from the kitchen toward Jagger. Pulling something from his apron.

The black cat hunched back, gathering himself. He hurtled at the concierge. Landed with legs straight out on the man's crotch and dug in with his claws. Bit. Hard. The man screeched. Backed up fast. Beating at the cat. The cat screamed a war cry and bit again.

More cats dashed in from the night.

Marconi siblings raced in, all behind the man, knocked into him, tripped over him, spreading out into a wedge. Falling. Rolling. Banging into tables. Cats and humans screeching.

My weapons were already in my hands. Without thinking, I had moved, crouching behind the low wall at my side.

Our bodyguard appeared from the darkness, kneeling, taking cover behind the wall at the door, holding it open, his weapon sweeping for a target. More armed protectors gathered there.

Cupcake ducked behind me.

Dishes clattered. People screamed. Diners raced into the night followed by their bodyguards.

The Marconi boys rolled on the floor, drawing knives and guns. Scooting into firing positions.

Jagger had drawn two weapons from God-knew-where. Aimed one at the brothers. The other through the open window into the kitchen, at the chef, Old Marconi. My bodyguard stood up behind him, one weapon aimed at the brothers, one at Jagger. "He's ours," I shouted to the bodyguard.

Cupcake had whipped out a tiny pistol from her cleavage and another from her hip.

Marconi's injured son screamed so high it hurt my ears. The black cat screeched again and tore for the door like a flying shadow.

The cat was gone, but the man covered his privates. There were long bloody scratches on his arms and hands. Thank goodness the black cat wasn't a queen. Unlike Tuffs, back at the scrapyard, he couldn't transmit nanos.

I dropped low, scooting on my toes into a better firing angle. I glanced back to see Cupcake in my peripheral vision. Returned my eyes to the doorway and Jagger. Remembered Spy's vision of the motorcycles.

MS Angels? Maybe tracking Jagger? He would be an enemy the Angels would know. But why did the Marconis—

The injured son curled into a ball, his screams going silent in agonized gasping.

"He's the top OMW enforcer," one of the Marconi daughters yelled from behind me.

"I'll put a pretty little hole in your pretty little eye, bitch," Cupcake said, her tiny pistol aimed in steady hands. "You take care of the others. I got the chick," she said, I assumed to Jagger and me.

Where had Cupcake's panicked tears from the morning gone to?

Old Marconi shouted from the kitchen, "My friends. My friends. No violence in my establishment."

Into the odd silence after Marconi's words, Jagger spoke. "I just wanted some nice Italian," he said, sounding reasonable and calm, despite the weapons, one of which was still centered on Old Marconi, as the man wandered from the kitchen, deceptively calm. "Maybe have a nice conversation with you, the Charleston chapter president of the Hells Angels, over a nice bottle of wine. I thought we could talk about the *Mara Salvatrucha*, working their way into the area, taking out the competition, see if there was any interest in working together for a little while. The enemy of my enemy and all that shit." Jagger grinned at Marconi. "In my jacket pocket I have four Montecristo cigars. The real thing. From Cuba. A peace offering."

Old Marconi looked around at his empty restaurant. "You could have asked," he said. "Call me. Send a little a note. You didn't have to ruin my night's business or castrate my heir. He's a good a boy." He flapped his hands at his family. "Put it away. I don't want to clean up blood tonight. Gunfights make such a mess."

"Papa," the girl behind me warned.

Marconi sent her a look. Then back to Jagger. "These women are yours?"

"No. I don't own women. Think of it like two birds, one stone. I get a nice meal as well as a nice chat with the Chapter prez. An important man. And maybe I get lucky after."

I narrowed my eyes at Jagger. Who was now officially back to being called Asshole.

"Four Montecristos?" Marconi asked.

"Limited editions. Two for us to enjoy after the meal, and two to leave with you as a gift."

"And my patrons?"

"Marconi's is too delightful for anyone to stay away," Jagger said, "though I do offer my sympathies for tonight's lost business. It's my hope our discussion will make up for it in some small way."

"We shall see." Marconi waved at his children again. "Seat our guest. Clean up the mess. Bring a decent bottle of wine and a nice salad for me. We will share a meal with your lovely ladies. We will talk. And we will decide what to do about the *Mara Salvatrucha*."

"Forgive me for saying, but if we discuss the MSA, we need to discuss the men your son Enrico met with this afternoon."

Old Marconi leveled his dark eyes at one of the men on the floor. He was a very pretty boy, the prettiness marred by anger and discontent. Slowly, Marconi said, "Enrico. What have you done?"

"The only thing I could, Papa." The boy climbed to his feet. He looked earnest and fearful at once, a handgun in each hand, street-thug style.

I tensed again and eased into a better firing position, my weapons on the boy, point-and-shoot style. Behind me, Cupcake said, "Uh-uh-uh. Weapon down, bitch. Or we'll bloody up your daddy's clean floors, starting with you."

"The world is changing," Enrico said. "We have to change with it."

The girl behind me shifted into view, her weapon —a lovely prewar H&K nine-millimeter—aimed at her brother. That was a surprise. She said, "The *Mara Salvatrucha* treat their women as slaves. I won't be some man's play toy." She was beautiful, and for reasons I didn't understand, I was reminded of the naked woman in the log mansion. And then it hit me. Was it possible that I had come into contact with MS Angels already? *Bloody damn*. I needed a private word with Asshole, but I wasn't going to get it.

"Lorenzo," Marconi said, "take Enrico's weapons. Secure his hands. Mina, remove and explore his Morphon. Download his contacts and locations to mine. There will be no slavery in my city. Children, put away your weapons. You too, lovely ladies who are my guests. You are under my protection. You others, serve the nice gentleman and the pretty ladies. And bring me a glass of the Elijah Craig, small batch. Get your brother to a med-bay, and call your mother. She will want to be here for this."

Jagger's weapons had already disappeared. I nodded to our bodyguard. The man shook his head, his expression saying it was part of his job to endure crazy stuff. He disappeared and the door swept closed, two cats racing out at the last moment. The others disappeared under tables; one hopped into the rafters as if an eight-foot jump were nothing. Spy. I got a whirlwind view of the restaurant and caught the low wall for balance before working my weapons back through my pockets. Cupcake's disappeared into her cleavage and elsewhere. I feared she would shoot herself, but when she plopped back into her chair, she smiled happily.

Swallowing my adrenaline and nanobot combat chemicals, I sat. Drank the rest of my beer. Wished for another. Miraculously one appeared at my place.

I should have been nauseated and shaky from the fight-or-flight breakdown chemicals. Instead, I was starving. I sipped, trying to remember the proper protocol. I had watched enough of such meetings when Pops was alive to know that specific things had to be said and done at the negotiating table. Old Ladies and random women were not allowed to participate unless they were spoken to first. Only made-men were permitted to speak, and it was best this family didn't know who I was.

Old Marconi sat, and a fifth chair appeared at his side, I assumed for his wife. I was interested to see what her status was. When she appeared in the kitchen, I realized that she had already been on the premises or she lived near the restaurant. I finally took a good look at the family. Old Marconi's skin—wrinkled, nearly as dark as mine, spotted with age—had seen a lot of sun and gravity. He sported a small beard and moustache, both pure white, while his hair was thick, white sprinkled with black, styled long, and swept back. He was justifiably proud of his hair. He had likely been killer pretty when he was younger, like Enrico, but his sharp black eyes said he had never been stupid. His daughter, Mina, took after her father.

"Mina. Did you know your brother had been talking to the *Mara Salvatrucha*?"

"No papa. I would have killed him myself had I known."

"This family and this chapter will never join with the *Mara Salvatrucha*. We will fight them until we die, as we always have. You will discover if any of your siblings or cousins or cohorts were part of his betrayal. And you will bring them to me. You will not kill them until I have dealt my own justice."

Mina snarled but spat, "Yes, Papa." She took Enrico's Morphon and hooked it to hers. Turning, she stared daggers at her brothers, one who was being helped to the back by another sister. She snarled again. Mina was vicious and unforgiving of any weakness. I filed that away. I might need it someday.

Marconi's Old Lady sat, ponderously, as if her knees hurt. Proving her status as a made-man, she said, "Give our guests decent wine." She held up her glass, and one of her sons filled it from a very large bottle of red, before replacing Cupcake's and Jagger's glasses with fresh ones, and filling them as well. She frowned mightily at the sight of my beer, but I stared her down. She did an eyebrow shrug, as if to say, *Oh well. The strange woman is a guest. She can drink what she wishes.* Another daughter placed a short rocks glass beside the Old Man and poured three fingers from a fancy whiskey bottle, no ice. At a gesture, the girl placed a matching glass at Jagger's side and poured an equal amount, also neat. The Old Lady held up her glass and said, "To information exchanged and peace in our city." We all clinked. Sipped. Set down our glasses.

Three Marconis stepped back but didn't depart. Still in earshot, they listened and watched us avidly. The Old Lady said, "I am Lucretia. My husband, Daniel Marconi."

Jagger said, "Logan Jagger." He pointed to me.

"Heather Anne Jilson. My mother was an Outlaw Old Lady before the war."

Jagger pointed at Cupcake.

"You can call me Cupcake. I used to be Red's Old Lady, with the original Hell's Angels. I stayed with him after the *Mara Salvatrucha* took over our chapter."

And then it hit me. Cupcake had all the contact info for every single MS Angels chapter. That meant she also knew which Hell's Angels chapters were still independent and fighting against the invading MS-13. She had known about the Marconis. *Cupcake* had made the reservations for us. *Cupcake* had arranged for Jagger to come here. I shot Cupcake a look, but she didn't return it, her eyes on Marconi.

Bloody damn hell.

"I remember Red," Marconi said. "He rode a Harley Bronx when I knew him. His old lady was comms and records specialist for the president of the Hell's Angels before the war. Red was number three. You left him?" He didn't move, but suspicion and threat laced his tone. "Where's Red?"

Bloody damn. Red had been the Hell's Angels' number three?

Cupcake said, "A female made-man, Clarisse Warhammer, moved up the roster at the national chapter house. When she hit number two, she was offered a chapter of her own, mostly to keep her from challenging the president. She took over our chapter. Red was knocked from chapter prez and from number three nationally to number four." Cupcake's eyes went hard as blue diamonds. "Clarisse made stupid decisions. Red died in a stupid-ass, ill-chosen MS Angels battle against superior forces. Warhammer and One-Eyed Jack ran off and *left her people to die*."

Cupcake didn't sound remotely like herself. Cupcake sounded like what she really was, an in-charge woman who took no guff from anyone. Cupcake was a dangerous badass and I hadn't known. *Bugger*.

She added, "Latest intel says she challenged the prez anyway, and he bugged out of St. Louis to a safe house somewhere."

I glanced at Cupcake. Mateo had picked up something about that possibility, but it hadn't been confirmed. I also hadn't shared it with Cupcake. More evidence my thralls were working behind my back. Good.

Jagger sipped his whiskey. "Very nice," he said of the liquor. "Clarisse Warhammer's chapter went up against me and a few of my people. When we found Cupcake, she was shot all to hell. We got her to a med-bay. Cupcake came over to our side to get away from the *Mara Salvatrucha*."

Marconi looked at Cupcake. Both of his hands were beneath the table. I didn't have to look around to know we were once again targeted. "You gave to our enemies all the contact information? You are a traitor?"

"No. She didn't. We didn't even know who she was until today," Jagger said. "But when she heard that the MS Angels were heading here from Louisville, she contacted me, to tell me there were a few honorable Angels fighting the good fight. We met today at the library and arranged to meet here, at your restaurant." Jagger looked at Cupcake. "You could have told me Marconi was your contact."

"You could have told both of us," Marconi said. "Perhaps my son would not be injured."

"Or perhaps we'd all be dead," Cupcake said.

I was clearly the least important person in the

group. That anonymity might keep me safe, which should suit me just fine. Should. Didn't. Ego and pride waggled around in my gut, emotions left over from being Little Girl, the daughter of the head of the Outlaws, and then a twelve-year-old female made-man in the war. A hero in my own right, promoted after I crawled into a Mama-Bot, disabled it, and survived, saving Outlaw chapter members, a buttload of military, and an entire city of civilians. Yeah. I had been important.

Which I couldn't share because I was important enough to go to war over. *This sucked*.

"It is a sin to let good food grow cold. Eat," Lucretia said.

Miraculously, my food was still warm, kept that way by a heated metal plate. It was spectacular. Better than anything Mateo could cook. Better than anything Cupcake could cook. I ate everything, ignoring the small talk around me and being ignored in return. But I discovered I didn't like being ignored, no matter how good the food. I drank two more beers. I may have sulked. When dessert came, it was little tarts with fresh fruit on them. Again, marvelous. The small talk stopped when Daniel Marconi looked at his Morphon and said, "My daughter informs me that her brother has been in contact with a woman in a hotel in Louisville. He promised to give her access to me. To his own father."

That meant the son had plotted patricide.

"Mina, come to the dining room."

Mina walked in. There was fresh blood on her white apron. I was pretty sure the blood was her brother's.

Daniel looked at his wife. "I know you love him best."

"I love all my children. Equally," she said, her eyes hard and dry but her lips quivering at the obvious lie. "Enrico has put this family and this city in danger. He will stand trial. Meanwhile," she asked Mina, "when was the betrayal to take place?"

"In two days. We have enemies close by." Mina looked at us. At Cupcake. "I don't believe in coincidence. Red's Old Lady is here today, on the eve of a war with the MSA? Looking us over? Maybe taking back info to the MS Angels? And him? The top enforcer in the OMW?"

She snarled again, clearly her preferred expression, and I could see her desire to kill us in her eyes. She was still and unmoving, loose and ready. This girl *was* a killer. Clearly a trained one. An assassin? Or a psychopath? Both?

"Forgive me for speaking," I said. "I'm not just a—civilian. I . . ."

I looked around and everyone was staring at me, some in reevaluation, one in threat. Jagger and Cupcake were waiting, giving me the chance to stay safe or take a part in whatever was happening here. An equal part. Out in the open. Or maybe partway in the open. I didn't want to create another thrall. But if I could keep the kid alive and that cemented a relationship that saved Charleston, that would be worth it.

"Speak," Old Man Marconi said.

"Clarisse Warhammer has a weapon she uses to control people." I stopped, thinking about what I was going to do and say. I found a partial truth and threaded the needle with it. "She puts a chemical on a teacup, a doorknob, a lowball glass." I glanced at Old Marconi's glass. "It enters through their skin. Or sometimes she uses a direct touch, a handshake, and it enters through a scratch or a tiny cut somewhere. That chemical makes them something like a slave."

"This Warhammer *drugged my son*?" Lucretia murmured. There was something dark in her eyes, something that said Mina had taken after her mother more than her father. But there was also hope there, that her son had not been a willing traitor.

I looked at Cupcake, who nodded slightly, as if she knew what I was doing and asking.

Cupcake said, "Warhammer is immune to the drug. She enslaved Red and me, and kept applying the drug. But the effects decrease if it isn't reapplied." Cupcake grinned at me. "Heather devised a med-bay program and has some Berger-chip plug-ins that make it easier to break the compulsion." She raised her eyebrows, making a point. "It's the only med-bay in the world that can break this compulsion."

Partial truth. Good enough.

"My son did not plot against this family by his own choice?" Lucretia demanded.

"Yes and no," Cupcake said. "When Warhammer transitioned Red and me, we knew right from wrong, but we didn't have any options, no way to get away. No one to help us. Your kid knew right from wrong. He still did wrong, even when he was away from her. He might be a weak person who followed the compulsion, like a sleepwalker in a dream, or he might be evil. I can't tell you that."

Lucretia glared at Cupcake. Cupcake shrugged. "I don't know your son."

"Did Enrico go away and come back recently?" I asked. "And has he been sick? Feverish, like the flu but worse. Sweating, maybe delirious."

"Yes," Lucretia said. "He had a sickness last week. A high fever. I feared we would all become sick, but no one did. Only Enrico."

"Fever is one sign of the toxin. He likely met with Warhammer seventy-two hours before that," I said. "And anything he touched before he washed his hands and clothes could have been transferable." I could feel Jagger's eyes on me in accusation as my words reminded him of his accidental transition. "If an employee or a chapter member touched his things right away, that person might be sick too."

Lucretia said, "We will make inquiries. Anyone who has had a fever will be quarantined."

Mina said, "The woman he met in Louisville. He says he's in love with her."

"Did he describe her?" I asked.

"Augmented. Meter and a half tall. Moves fast. Pretty." Mina placed a Morphon on the table and touched it open. It displayed a series of photos. "Is this the woman who poisoned my brother?"

"Yes," Jagger said.

"You can cure my son?" Lucretia asked me.

"I can try. It might kill him." I looked at Cupcake. "She made it sound easy. It wasn't. She nearly died."

"True," Cupcake said with a saucy grin.

"Warhammer has some of our people," Jagger said. He put down his glass and leaned forward, elbows on the table. It was earnest body language, saying he was showing all his cards. "She's entrenched, well-funded, and she's made contact with and likely converted a group of military and Gov. employees at the state and national level. She's making an army with that chemical. We're going after her before she takes over completely. We're getting our people back and taking out Warhammer and all her slaves."

"Except for my son. You want something from us," Daniel said, sipping his whiskey, holding the glass one-handed near his chin and breathing in the fumes. "What?"

Jagger looked at me. "Tell 'em."

Because Jagger knew I was here for something, but I hadn't told him what. *Right.* "We're here to get a weapon, currently buried in the ground. A wartime weapon. We need to get it without the Law or the Gov., who might be in Warhammer's pockets, learning about it. We need a distraction. A big one. And we need an earthmover, front-end loader-dozer combo if possible. Or a backhoe, any heavy-duty excavation equipment you might have access to, and a large-capacity pump in case we hit water."

"My people can provide this. But we want the weapon."

Jagger grinned and sat back, taking his glass with him. He sipped his whiskey, considering the older couple. "Once we're finished taking down Warhammer, you can try to take it away from us. But then Heather won't try to cure your kid."

Old Marconi pursed his lips as if thinking, but his

black eyes were shining with something I understood completely. It was the expression some people wore when bargaining. I saw it a lot at the scrapyard. "I could take the woman," he said, looking at me. "Force her to give us her med-bay and save my son. Take the weapon. Leave you with no help."

"I didn't bring it with me," I said, letting only a hint of scoffing into my tone. I didn't need to tick him off. Yet. And maybe not at all. "Why would I? I didn't know about your son or how he betrayed his family."

Marconi's eyes narrowed, as if insulted. I just grinned. I'd played this game for years, and Old Marconi's lips pursed as if he recognized that. He also seemed to know I had more cards against my chest than it first appeared, that *I* was more than I appeared. He said slowly, "I will provide this distraction. I will arrange to have earthmovers available, free of charge, a sign of good will. I will leave the weapon to you, and will not go to war with you, *if* my son survives. Assuming you win this weapon and the war against this Warhammer, and again assuming my son survives, what do I get in return?"

"Assumptions don't work," I said. "Here's the facts. You'll never see Warhammer's chemical delivered. You'll just see your children and your chapter get sick, and some of your people will die as the chemical takes over. The ones who survive will change overnight, like Enrico did. Your life as you know it will end, and you'll never see it coming."

I set my stein down and leaned in. "That said, you work with us, and in return for your help we'll *fight your war for you*. We will remove a dire threat to your chapter and your family. You don't have to send your children to fight an enemy they will never see coming. Also, I'll *attempt* to save your son and any of your people affected. *Attempt*. Nothing guaranteed. That's it. Take it or leave it."

"This woman speaks for you?" Marconi asked Jagger, his tone insulting.

"We take it," Lucretia said to him.

Marconi shrugged with his whole body and face. "The mother of my children has spoken. In matters of family she is fully in charge."

"Oh," I said. "One more thing. There's a cost to the cure. I'll need specific Berger plug-ins, and since they go into your son's brain, you'll want to provide them. That way there aren't any trust issues."

"You are young to have such medical training," Marconi said. Unsaid was, *and negotiating skill*.

I met Old Man Marconi's black eyes and said flatly, "Battlefield training."

He nodded at what that meant and who I might be. Not a nobody. He raised his voice. "Do I smell coffee from Bolivia? Not that cheap swill we serve the patrons?"

"Yes, Papa," one of the boys who had been listening said. The boy raced to the kitchen and returned with a tray, set with a white cloth, a thermal coffee server, and five tiny cups. "Espresso," the boy said, reverently. I hadn't had espresso in . . . since before the war. The boy placed a delicate sugar and creamer set on the table, with five small white napkins and five sterling spoons. Into the five tiny white cups he poured black espresso, the coffee steam aromatic enough to make me want to weep for the lost past.

I accepted the small cup. It would keep me up all night. I didn't care. I took mine black. Breathed in the steam. Sipped. Raised my eyes to Jagger and gave a faint nod.

"I'm in agreement in principle," Jagger said, taking the tiniest sip.

"I too have one more thing," Daniel said, sounding almost lazy. "You will take one of my sons and train him for a period of one year. Then you will return him in good health and alive."

Jagger frowned, and I knew that bargaining expression too. It meant a deal-breaker had just been laid on the table. "With all the secrets of the Outlaws? No."

"Reconsider."

"Personal assistant to the enforcer?" Jagger asked. "Dangerous job for a kid who would also be a hostage. I'm not a babysitter to keep a pup alive."

Marconi shrugged slightly, but as a bargaining gesture, not speaking the truth. "All of life is dangerous, and I have many sons."

Lucretia shot daggers at her husband, but he kept talking.

"All are capable in a fight, in a negotiation, on a bike. However, all of them, especially Enrico, are precious to their mother. You will heal Enrico and return him. If he does not return in one piece as outlined"—he shrugged again, that sparkle bright in his clever eyes—"I will declare war on the Outlaws and personally on the enforcer to the vice president, *McQuestion*."

Laying out the Outlaw command structure and using the pseudonym "McQuestion" indicated Marconi knew a lot about the Outlaws. "You will also take one of my sons and train him at your side. Those are my conditions for my help."

Jagger sipped, closed his eyes in happiness at the taste. Opened them and focused on Marconi. "These are conditions I will take upline. The hostage will wear an Outlaw Morphon instead of his own. If he dies by his own stupidity, in an accident, in any way that I can't control, there will be proof. And there will be no war, no repercussions for any act of God or boyhood stupidity." He shrugged. "All boys have stupid moments."

Marconi said, "He can call home. Talk to his mother. His brothers and sisters."

"Supervised calls. Trip home for Christmas if you pay for transportation costs."

"Agreed. And I will provide funds to supplement his food for one year."

Jagger grinned again, showing strong teeth, finally getting deeply into the bargaining. "Food *and* water. Weapons, ammo, bike, gas, and repairs. And one pound of roasted coffee beans, unground, this brand, every quarter. And, of course, McQuestion may have conditions as well."

The Marconis looked at each other, their eyes saying so much. "Deal," they said together.

"Deal," Jagger said. They clicked glasses. "Which kid?"

"Jacopo."

The boy serving the espresso nearly dropped the carafe. His eyes went wide. "I will bring honor to my family and to the Charleston chapter." They were formal words, similar to one of the vows new Outlaws swore before they were confirmed. The kid should be too young to be a made-man, but the war had changed everything. I received my battlefield Outlaw patch and tattoo at age twelve. Jacopo was being offered a great honor and responsibility—and being placed in danger. He was all in. I had a feeling he was a full chapter member. Marconi clearly had big plans for this kid.

Jacopo turned to Jagger. "I will bring honor to the enforcer of McQuestion."

Marconi said, "You will go with your brother to this woman's med-bay and confirm your brother's safety. Then you will join the enforcer."

Bugger. I figured I had a good chance to keep the sick kid blindfolded for the ride to the scrapyard, but keeping a healthy one in the dark was a lot harder. Marconi would know where I live. Mateo would have a meltdown.

Jagger frowned. "You ride?"

Jacopo's white teeth flashed. "I'm the best on a bike in the entire family. I'm next to Mina with knives and weapons. I have the highest IQ."

"And the least modesty of all my children," Lucretia said, her words dripping sarcasm.

"You patched?" Jagger asked.

The room went still. I caught a flash of Spy's face overhead. She was staring at Jacopo as if she wanted him to pet her. Or as if she wanted to eat his dead body. Hard to tell which.

Jacopo glanced at his parents and his father gave a scant nod. His mother frowned. "Yes. In the interests of full disclosure, my first two kills were from a night that armed intruders tried to get in the house. I was ten." Jacopo's face went hard, and it was clear he was no longer bragging. He was stating facts about something that had marked him deeply. "Our babysitter was killed when they entered from an upstairs bedroom window. She fought hard, and it bought me the time I needed to make it downstairs to the gun safe. Papa didn't know I knew the combination. One intruder died on the stairs. The other one made it to the main level."

Lucretia and Daniel's fingers touched and laced together. The memory was painful to them all.

"Weapons?" Jagger asked, gently.

"Nine mils. I wasn't a good shot. They had to patch up the walls. In the last five years, I got better." Jacopo's face was a stone, and he looked older than his fifteen years. "Now I don't miss. Ever."

I sighed and held the tiny cup in my gloved hands, sipping, thinking. He was fifteen and busting at the seams with piss and vinegar like some super teenage ninja who I had to protect from my own queen nanobots. *God help me.* Things were getting complicated.

The evidence I had with Mateo and Cupcake suggested that being inundated with Berger chips didn't destroy the nanobots, but the overload of info did rewire the victims' brains, giving them an increasing freedom of choice.

Jagger still needed more Berger chips. A lot more. Either that, or his own attraction to me was keeping him in thralldom. So far, setting him free was a failure. If Jacopo were accidently transitioned, I could get my people killed.

It was midnight, but we were too coffee-wired to go to sleep. When you haven't had good coffee in years and you drink two cups of espresso, it jumpstarts your body like an anti-grav grabber. You feel like you're floating, vibrating, and you have to move. So Jagger, our bodyguard, Cupcake, five cats, and I ordered a rental car recommended by Marconi (which meant he likely owned a percentage of the company) and drove to see the earthmover he had reserved for us. We were exceptionally well-dressed visitors to the equipment yard, but no one said anything about the strappy heels and the dresses, not after Marconi's call and approval. We traipsed across dry rutted ground to the earthmover, and Jagger looked it over.

Half a century ago, it was the latest model, one designed to use a variety of shovels, buckets, snowplow, moldboard, and grader. The paint was long gone, but the mechanics and hydraulics looked well maintained, and the bucket was new and not missing teeth. In a shed nearby was a high-capacity pump, which came with a bladder system, and Jagger seemed to know why that was important and how to use it. He and Cupcake and the bodyguard—I finally learned his name was Amos—had a long conversation about the equipment and its limitations and strengths. I listened and learned a lot about bladders, valves, gear boxes, and hydraulics. It was information a scrapyard owner and any warrior might need.

We got back to the hotel before 2:00 a.m., sent Amos off, and we three curled up on the sofa and the chair, with the cats running everywhere, mock hunting. Together we went over prewar city maps and new maps, and discussed getting the machines to the swamp where the Simba was buried. I hadn't seen wetlands in years and was looking forward to it.

At breakfast, I would be bargaining for the rest of the equipment we needed to rescue the battle tank. We needed my trades with Morrison's Foundry, Metals, and Scrap to provide us with a single piece of military equipment that a snoop from Harlan's old network had suggested Morrison possessed. A rare, hard to turn over, and very expensive piece of equipment that fell off an Army truck—meaning it was stolen.

Marty Morrison was a sneaky bastard. I had to be on my toes.

So of course, I crashed at 4:00 a.m. I never heard Jagger leave.

The only good thing about the busy night and the crash was that Jagger's afternoon kiss and its promise of mind-blowing sex went nowhere. Which was good. Because I had already surely reinfected Jagger by sticking my tongue down his throat.

There was no espresso to wake me up. Jagger did that by banging on our door. It was so loud the hotel patrons up the hall shouted in irritation.

Cupcake and I got fast showers—God, I loved water!—smeared on sunscreen, dressed in sun-protective clothing and gear, grabbed weapons, and headed into the day. Jagger was in the hotel's secure parking area, sitting on his anonymous bike beside the big rig. Amos was standing beside him, carrying a rifle, a shotgun, two handguns, and a daypack. When Cupcake maneuvered the huge diesel onto the road, the bodyguard jumped into the bed and made himself comfy, protecting the trade items. I liked Amos. He was dependable, not trigger-happy, steady like a rock. And he brought his own guns.

Morrison's Foundry, Metals, and Scrap was on the other side of the river, and Cupcake maneuvered the rig over the rickety bridge like the pro she was, chattering incessantly. I was pretty sure that if I'd had coffee, I would feel less inclined to strangle her. Maybe.

Jagger followed us on his motorcycle, weaponed up like he was going to war, meaning he carried everything he owned that cut, sliced, diced, boiled people's innards, or went bang. At Morrison's, Cupcake pulled in where I instructed, and parked the rig while I fluffed my spiked hair, smeared on fresh lipstick, and prayed Marty would serve coffee with our breakfast.

I secured my weapons: a ten-millimeter strapped over my jeans at my left thigh, a .32 holstered at my spine over a T-shirt and under a loose cotton shirt, and a blaster holstered on my right thigh close beside my hand. I had done business at Morrison's four times in the past, but I'd never had a stack of sterling or the jewelry Cupcake had unearthed. I didn't want Marty to think I was a pushover, or that he could help himself, or about his profit margins if he ended us and dumped our bodies in a hole.

I pulled on thin leather gloves that covered my bicolor-ant scars and swung down from the cab. The cats dropped down after me. "As soon as you find the new containers, let me know," I said to Spy. "They'll smell different from containers that have been in the scrapyard for years. And watch out for junkyard dogs."

She tilted her head, clearly insulted that I thought she and her pals couldn't handle a dog or two. The cats scattered.

I tapped my comms and said quietly, "Mateo?" The *SunStar*'s EntNu communication system was handy in case we needed info not available on my outdated Berger chip. And in case Mateo had to mount a do-or-die rescue, giving away all our secrets and probably getting caught and stripped out of his warbot suit. Which would kill him. The last thing I wanted.

"Copy," his metallic voice said.

I walked around to the side of the truck bed and peered at Amos through the side slats. "Stay put. You hear shots, you protect the trade items. If there's a firefight and we get through this alive, your bonus will be nice. And stay out of the sun."

"Yes, ma'am." He grinned through a full beard, missing teeth attesting to his familiarity with fistfights, and popped open an umbrella I hadn't seen. He relaxed in its meager shade.

I met Jagger and Cupcake, adjusted my 2-Gen sunglasses, and tugged the gloves tighter for possible weapons draw. "Let's go have breakfast with Marty."

"Rock and roll," Cupcake said. She tossed the bag of jewelry she had brought to trade and caught it one-handed, before tying it to her belt at her split cotton skirt. She looked tough yet feminine, wearing biker boots, a plaid shirt tied at the waist, and Little Mama's old hat, which she had called a fancy Panama sunhat. She carried a sawed-off shotgun, one I hadn't seen before, and I started to tell her the recoil would knock her on her ass, but she did have my nanos. She probably could handle the recoil just fine.

I led the way to the front door of the sales room, smelling bacon and maple syrup on the air. Marty had never offered me breakfast before. Cupcake said, "By the way, I'm your security, personal secretary, and antiquities specialist. My job is to make sure you get the biggest bang for your buck. And keep Marty off-balance."

I chuckled. "Knock yourself out. He knows me as Ms. Smith. If you have to use a first name, go with Heather."

Cupcake entered—shotgun to the fore—and stepped to the left. I entered and stepped beside her. Jagger followed to the right and closed the door. After the bright daylight, the interior of Morrison's was blindingly dim. I pulled off my sunglasses, even my weird eyes needing light. The public area had been refloored, the walls painted, and a new sales counter installed. Three men stood behind it, two of them with weapons out. The one without a weapon drawn was Marty.

"Ms. Smith!" he called out, too loud, hale and hearty. "Just in time." He rounded the counter and indicated the small area to the right of the door. It had once been an octagonal nook with tall windows, but had been redecorated since my last visit, now with a round table and chairs, the windows draped. Marty pulled out a seat for me, one facing the windows, my back to the door. Cupcake slid around me and took up a position in an angle of the nook. She stared at Marty as she pulled out the chair in the most secure spot. Without a word, I took the seat she offered. Jagger moved across the room to a better firing angle. He could take down the armed men behind the counter, shoot Marty in the back, as well as cover the front door and the hallway leading into the back of the shop. Or he could stand there looking scary. Which he did.

I settled myself and said to Marty, "It smells divine. I was honored when my assistant said you invited me to breakfast." I pulled off the holster and blaster with a melodramatic relieved sigh and placed them on the table, inches from my plate. I smiled at Marty.

Marty Morrison had never seen my funky orange irises. They gave some people the willies. Marty stared at them, seeing the color, not me. I had considered that my weirdness might be useful. Seemed I was right.

Cupcake asked, "Breakfast first, or deals?"

Marty dragged his gaze to Cupcake, who had perfectly gorgeous but normal blue eyes. He frowned as if he felt something was wrong, but he couldn't say what. Then he flashed that salesman's smile I remembered from before and said, "Mix it up? A little show-and-tell, a little food, a little dickering."

"Fine," Cupcake said. Still keeping the shotgun aimed in the general direction of the armed men, she took the bag of goodies from her belt and placed it on the table. She loosened the drawstring and reached in, her fingers clinking around in the bag before removing a random gold wedding band encrusted with diamonds. My eyes nearly bugged out of their sockets. She tossed it to the center of the table where it rolled before stopping. "There's the show. The tell is a princess cut, colorless, white fluorescent, GIS flawless, two-carat center diamond, with two side-stone bullets of high-grade rubies mounted on a twenty-four-karat gold band." Cupcake scooped up the ring and deposited it in the bag, Marty following each movement with avarice in his eyes. "Now feed my boss lady. She gets ornery when she's hungry."

In my earbud, Mateo chuckled, the sound almost human. "She used new Berger chips. Cupcake's been studying your scrap."

Marty smiled again and said, "For us, waffles, real scrambled eggs, real bacon, real maple syrup. Egg-and-bacon sandwiches for the bodyguards. Coffee for everyone." He looked back at the armed men. "Notify Wanda we're ready." He took the dangerous seat, back to the door.

A moment later, a woman appeared carrying a tray, and she served our plates. My mouth watered. Wheat had taken a hurting when the atmosphere changed, and getting real bread, especially something fancy like waffles, was a rarity. While I felt guilty about feasting while my "employees" munched on sandwiches, it wasn't enough to stop my enjoyment.

When the meal was over and the only thing left was eggy, maple-y grease smeared on the plates, Cupcake placed the bag of goodies in my hand.

I shoved my plate to the center and weighed the clinking bag hand-to-hand, thinking about all the sheds and containers Cupcake had been inventorying. Thinking about the cats outside looking for the piece of equipment I needed and hoped Marty had. I watched Marty's eyes as they darted from mine to the bag and back. Wanda removed the plates. The office went quiet except for the soft clink of jewelry. I waited.

"I liked the ring," Marty said. "Two hundred US for it."

I chuckled, the bag moving. Still waiting.

"Three hundred," he said.

I counted four clinks before I said, "I'm not interested in money. I want something you might have in trade."

"Yeah?" Marty leaned back. Trade meant off the books. Trade meant no taxes, no records. Trade meant possibly, potentially, *likely*, illegal items changing hands. "I might consider trade."

I thought about Spy and gripped the table to control my reaction. *You see anything?*

She sent back a dizzying array of sheds and locked shipping containers. I spotted a repainted one, camo brown over military green, and sent her that way. If Marty had what I needed, it would have been overpainted. Spy and the other cats zeroed in and began to search for a way in, clawing at rusty corners, vaulting to the top.

I opened the bag and started to reach in, then stopped. "Do the honors?" I asked Cupcake. Since I had no idea what was inside, that seemed wise. She retook the bag and removed the original ring. Marty accepted it and pulled a jeweler's loupe from a pocket. I had never used a loupe, but Marty was clearly an expert, his hands braced on each other to steady the ring and loupe, minuscule movements back and forth and side to side to get a good angle. When he was done, he leaned back in his chair and looked unimpressed, except for a faint uncontrolled gleam in his eyes. Cupcake took the ring back and returned the bag to her belt.

"What else you got?" he asked.

"The man isn't interested in jewelry," I said. "Outside." I stood and had the pleasure of seeing Marty blink. He wanted to see more jewelry, so that would be the last thing I showed him.

The day's heat had multiplied into a vicious miasma of junkyard stinks: old petrol, burnt motor oil, hot steel, rotting rubber, caustic substances, and dog poo. That was one problem with most junkyards, the dogs. Cats buried their scat, so the stench was less potent. Marty didn't clean up after his dogs, letting the waste dry in the heat. At least there was no hot-metal stink and exhaust from the foundry. The last time I was here they were pouring steel; the stench and heat had been astounding, rising in waves high over Morrison's. My Berger chip chirped, *Convection causes variations in the temperature of very hot air, and that variation—*

I shut it off. Pulled my glasses back over my eyes. "Amos?" I called. "The man's coming up. Unwrap the trays."

"Yes, ma'am," Amos called back. I heard him

moving around.

I gestured to Marty. "Help yourself."

He hesitated. "You left a guard?"

I tilted my head, saying nothing, letting the necessity of a guard—outside, in the heat—worm through Marty's head. It meant I had more good stuff to trade. I leaned against the rig's shady side as Marty pulled himself up into the bed and began to rummage around. He was noisy, the vibrations of his search shuddering through the vehicle. It took a long time. Scrawny, stinking junkyard dogs came and went, sniffing crotches, accepting treats from the guards, receiving a halfhearted kick or two from them when they got too personal. They ignored my crew and me, which was interesting. I was sweating like a stevedore, a sticky summer sweat, oily and slimy. I needed water. I had to pee.

Spy had wormed her way inside a container and sent me a vision of a box marked with a logo and words that meant nothing to her, but matched what Harlan had told me months ago had been delivered to Morrison's. It was the piece of equipment I needed to recover the Simba.

I sent back to her waves of delight, and if a cat could pat herself on the back, Spy would have. She returned to me a vision of a pile of sardines, protein, the only thing cats really cared about. Well, protein, toys, belly rubs, and, occasionally, something to kill.

I sent a vision of her outside, walking around the container and searching out symbols, and got back a vision of a human rolling in mud. I wasn't sure why. Then she sent me a vision of a corner of the desert-camo siding and a partially painted-over number: 814. I returned a vision of sardines and felt Spy's back arch with pleasure. The cat and I had struck a junkyard bargain.

Marty finally jumped to the ground and joined me in the shade, his eyes hard and uncompromising. Large sweat rings circled beneath his arms and along his back, the result of moving the heavy scrap to see the trays and the copper. "Okay," he said. "I saw the silver and the copper. Here's what I want. Everything in the truck except the crap scrap. I got enough of that to last me a lifetime. And I want the ring."

"For what?" I asked. "Cash? Or that trade I mentioned? Which we have not discussed."

"What do you want?" he snapped. Then caught himself and smiled.

I relaxed against the warm armored cab door and tapped my lips as if thinking. "Let's go for a walk. I'll pick a container."

"Fine."

I snapped my fingers to Cupcake, in a bossy gesture. "Add up the wholesale value of all our larger trade items. In case I see something I want."

I found Spy in my mind and located her general direction from the main office. Marty and I walked side by side, with Cupcake, Jagger, and Marty's two armed men behind us. Of the six of us, I had a feeling that Cupcake could become the most deadly of us all. What the hell had happened to the weepy woman who had killed her first man yesterday? Had the nanobots restructured her brain into what she thought I needed within hours of the battle? That was a terrifying possibility.

We wandered. I pointed to container 427 and looked inside when Marty opened the lock. I mentally catalogued the contents, shrugged, and pointed to container 212, and then 386, with the same results. For each container, Marty used the same master key. That was stupid.

A tortie cat dropped from a height and landed in front of us, looked at me, and sprang back up high, but down a narrow pathway to the right. I followed. Marty whipped his head at the cat's appearance, but said nothing. Cats kept down the rat population, and Marty likely had feral and stray cats all over. But this one was mine.

Down the narrow aisle, I saw a series of desert-camo-painted shipping containers, three of them six meters long, two of them twelve meters long. From the smell of fresh paint, lack of filth on them, and the deep truck-tire tracks in the dirt around the bases, it was clear these were new-ish. I wondered how Marty's military network had been put together. He was crossing dangerous lines.

I pointed at the first container and watched from the corner of my eye as Marty hesitated. Cupcake jingled the jewelry bag, an enticement.

Marty opened the odd, heavy lock. This key was different—thick and bulky, with both a male-female and female-male center part. I had a feeling it also involved a laser. Marty had military locks. Marty had gone into the black market big time. That meant the Hand of the Law had been bribed.

A thought squirreled under my breastbone. Harlan was always looking for military scrap.

Harlan was dead.

The container opened, a squeaking black maw. I stepped in. "Well, well, well," I said. "Marty's got him some weapons." My gaze swept over the military ordnance, counting. Twenty-five cases, each holding a minimum of three long-rifles capable of multiple-caliber projectiles, all with AI targeting and high-capacity mags. I heard multiple clicks from three different weapons, all behind me.

"Seriously, Marty?" Cupcake asked. "You're going to have a shoot-out right here? You three against us three? Even if you walk away from a firefight alive, Amos has orders to blow everything into next year. You'll get nothing, and your pretty new decorated office will be a pile of splinters. *And* the blast will bring law enforcement in from everywhere."

"Put away the weapons," I said, trying to sound grumpy instead of terrified. "No one is shooting anyone. I have customers who sometimes need military hardware. Now, I know where to send them." I turned around to see Marty a meter away, still pointing a blaster at my middle, his finger on the trigger that would cause my blood to boil. He looked uncertain, on the edge, and I decided he needed a little push in the right direction. It was dark enough that he might not realize I was moving too fast to be human.

I ducked. Swiveled. Kicked. My heel whacked Marty's hand. The blaster went flying.

He gave a yodel of pain.

Cupcake grabbed the blaster out of the air. Pointed it at Marty.

Jagger was suddenly *there*, in the doorway, two weapons pointing at the heads of the armed men. All of us, faster than human.

"Really, boys," Jagger drawled, his accent extra strong. "You don't wanta do that."

Marty flexed his hand. "You could have broken my hand."

"Could have. Didn't. Let's move on. I'm not interested in fully automatic rifles, even if they *do* have third-gen targeting systems." I meandered outside and to container number 814. Stood in the agonizing heat, waiting. Eventually Marty unlocked the steel door. I stepped inside. Looked around, bored. Then I stopped. "Marty, is that a second-generation Tesla Lockmart IGP?" I bent into a squat in front of the box. "I might be interested in this little baby, assuming the price is right."

Marty was suddenly the salesman again, holding his bruised hand, unctuous, and willing to do business. "Newest version of the Antigravity Grabber," he said. "Half the size of the original model, with nearly twice the lifting power. Portable. Self-propelled, easy to pilot, turns on a dime. I got two of these beauties, and these babies can be run on multiple fuel and power sources. Idiot-proof operating system. Even come with battery backup, so you don't lose whatever you're holding during unexpected power outages. Both are for sale." He patted the container and indicated a box behind the one I could see.

"Mmm. I can see how a portable one might come in handy. You ever used one?"

"I have one in the foundry. Useful lil' sucker."

I stood dusting off my gloved hands. "Yeah. Maybe. Let's see some more."

A successful bargain was based on the tickle and grab, or the bait and hook. It required a buyer to show just enough interest to make the seller think they might have a sale, then walk away. Then mention that item. Then walk away. It required the buyer (me) to make the seller (Marty) want to make the deal, make him think he's pulling one over on me if I'm interested. Of course, the seller was playing the same game in reverse, but that just made it more interesting. Especially when there were weapons in play.

I made Marty show me all the other camo-painted containers, and I picked three different items, including a high-tech microscope that could be used for geological specimens, metallurgy, and biology, depending on the oculars and the digital software. I also found a top-of-the-line automatic-targeting scope I could mount on top of the office and tie into the security system, and a new refrigeration unit I could sell in a heartbeat. We dickered. We cussed each other a little, called each other names as we stood in the heat and sweated. Marty wanted easily disposable and transportable jewelry, but the three items together weren't worth the ring. We agreed on four silver trays instead.

We headed back to my truck, me with a bounce in my step as if I had what I wanted. Marty a little slower, pondering his next negotiating move.

We watched as Marty's men unloaded my scrap, the good-quality stuff and the worthless stuff that would go back on the truck to cover up my purchases. I watched as my three new items were placed and secured in the truck bed.

And then Marty, oh so casually, took the bait. "You still interested in that Tesla Lockmart IGP? A portable AG Grabber is worth its weight in gold."

I nearly bit my cheek trying to hold in my victory grin. "I have plenty of gold. And I already have an IGP."

"An old one, right? Original year?"

"Yeah. So?" I asked, a little belligerent.

"They don't even make parts for original models these days. I'd love to close a deal with you on one of the IGPs."

I shrugged and accepted a drink from Marty's henchman. Their weapons were all hidden now, so that meant things were progressing nicely. Time for the Bargaining Dance. I tilted back the drink and discovered it was cola. I hadn't had a cola in ages. It bubbled and burned and went down so sweet I nearly wanted to cry. "Been a while since I had one of these," I said. "Nice. But I don't know, Marty. Just because I'm flush now, doesn't meant I will be later. I might need other things before I need an IGP."

"I've been known to work with people who fell on hard times. Make some deals between friends."

"Work *with* people?" I let him see my teeth in what only a magnanimous person would call a smile. "I've heard the tales about your goons working *on* people. With baseball bats."

"Don't believe everything you hear, Shining." He placed a hand over his heart. "I'm mighty easy to work with. Mighty easy. Make me an offer."

Shining.

I went cold and hard and eternally *pissed*. Things I had hoped were not true, but clearly were, settled inside me. I squinted at Cupcake. "That ring is worth way more than a piece of equipment we don't need."

Cupcake was watching me, her eyes taking in the tiny, intimate body-language changes only a thrall would see. To Marty, she said, "Toss in some seeds. I saw packets of heirloom seeds behind the counter. And we could use some solder to seal the rain catcher."

"Soldering iron I might could use," I said, working things through, "but still not value for value."

"Tell you what," Marty said. "You give me that ring, and one other ring of my choosing, and I'll load up an IGP, a top-of-the-line, heavy-duty soldering station and iron, new in the box, extra solder, an old but operational M72 laser, and I'll keep a credit on the books."

M72? Dayum! I frowned a little. "Nah. Cash I'm willing to do. Not credit. Sorry, Marty." I raised my voice. "Okay, people. Time to head out."

"I can do cash," Marty said quickly.

I made a face and rocked my head side to side as if thinking. "A girl can always use liquid assets." I glanced around and didn't see Jagger or the cats. Marty's men still had their weapons holstered. "I guess we can chat about it. But I'm not paying top dollar for something I don't need today."

Marty grinned and we both looked at Cupcake. She frowned, not certain where I was going or what I might want her to do. She settled on hefting the bag, which clinked temptingly. "I'll show you six rings, all fourteen karat. Your choice of the original and one other."

"Deal," Marty said. He looked at me. "She's cute. You two . . . you know . . ." He made an obscene gesture.

Cupcake burst out laughing and pulled herself onto the truck's running board, moving faster and smoother as the nanobots in her system prepared her body for battle. She opened the driver's door and hot air whooshed out. She scooted across and opened the passenger door, too, before she dropped to the ground. "It's hot. Let's go inside where it's cool and I can pick out my seeds." She led the way to Marty's storefront, business office, and breakfast joint. "And another cola for the boss lady would be nice."

As we walked, I realized that Cupcake didn't look like Cupcake anymore. She looked younger, sprier, prettier. My nanobots had done what Clarisse Warhammer's hadn't. They were rebuilding her, healing age-related illnesses. Cupcake was mutating. Fast. And it had started yesterday. With gunfire.

While Cupcake handled the financial details, I watched the heavy gear being loaded. I had gotten everything I needed, a few things I could sell, a handful of cash, and everything Cupcake wanted, which meant a bag of seed packets and a batch of solar panels. Marty ended up with six trays and two rings: the flawless diamond-and-ruby ring and a gold band encrusted with five quarter-karat diamonds.

I checked on Amos, who was soaked in sweat and nearly prostrate with heat exhaustion after helping load and rearrange. There were a dozen empty water bottles on the floor near him and as many more full of pee. Smart man. "Anything?" I asked him softly.

"Yeah. Cats everywhere, and the woman made a tour of the rig. We chatted. I didn't see her plant anything, but I could have missed it."

"Copy." I tapped my earbud. "Mateo. You there?"

"Monitoring cameras and transmissions. The mini-cams caught it. Pull over when you cross the river and I'll direct you to two tailers." Tailers were tracking systems that could use vibrations, static electricity, or solar for power. Marty wanted to know where we were. Not unexpected after his slip. Marty wanted to—what? Find us and steal the goods back? Tell someone where we were?

"Let's take them off now," I murmured. "Before we leave."

"You sure? He's watching you."

"Yeah? Good. Marty needs a lesson that might make him bleed."

"What kind of lesson?" Mateo's mechanical voice was suspicious. "What did I miss?"

"Later. Amos," I said to the guard, "we're about to have trouble."

"Ten-four." Things moved around in Amos's hidey-hole as he maneuvered his weapons.

I raised my voice. "Asshole!"

Jagger walked around the corner of the building, a warrior ready for anything. He drew his weapons and stood with his back to the side of the business office. I didn't see the henchmen. Didn't mean they were taking naps. Didn't mean I wasn't being targeted.

Cupcake appeared, Marty close behind. Mateo told me where the two tailers were planted, and I bent under the diesel's running board for the first one and stopped at the rig's back tires for the second one. I stared at Marty and rattled the tailers in my closed fist. "Marty, Marty, Marty," I said, sounding sad, staring at him as I let my anger free.

Cupcake stepped into the cab and removed her handgun from the side pocket. Cats, sensing problems, came from everywhere. Two hurtled into the cab. The others scattered around, hunting, hiding.

Still sounding sad, I said, "You planned to use these tailers to track me? Take back all the items?" My voice got hard. "Go back on our deal? Maybe turn us over to the MS Angels?"

He raised his hands, all peaceable. "Ms. Smith, I'd never do such a thing. And I'd never do business with a gang."

I caught a vision from Spy. The two armed men were on the roof of the storefront. They were pointing weapons at us. I sent back a vision of Spy and some of the clowder leaping on top of the men, clawing, and taking a bite out of what skin was available. Instantly my vision scrambled into fractions of activity.

From the roof, a gunshot and a human scream rang out. Cat yowls. More screaming.

Marty froze at the sight of my blaster, suddenly in my hand. I was holding on to the truck cab with my other hand, dizzy, but not showing it.

Two dogs came running, all teeth and attitude, slavering, mistreated, trained to attack. I didn't have nonlethal weapons on me, but being pulled down and mauled wasn't on my dance card today. With my free hand, I pulled a handgun and aimed it at the closest dog.

A cat soared from the truck cab onto the dog and clawed in, biting down on his ear. The other cat landed on the second dog's nose.

I turned my extra weapon to Marty, who was, by

now, pointing a semiautomatic at me.

The dogs raced off, yelping. The cats disappeared.

"Oh, Marty," I made some little *tsking* sounds, my heartrate speeding, my breathing deepening.

The woman, Wanda, stepped from the office, quick like a snake, and shoved a weapon into Jagger's side. In my exact tone of voice, she said, "Oh, Ms. Smith."

They thought they had us.

Faster than human, Jagger stepped in a sinuous "S" shape around her weapon. He batted her gun away and snatched her in front of him, his nine-millimeter at her chest.

Marty swung his weapon to the woman and back to me, his mouth slightly open. Scant seconds had passed since the start of the attack. I smiled again, the nasty smile.

Spy sent me a vision of two men on the roof, scratched and bleeding, their weapons to the side. One of the men was crying, a hand over his eye. I figured he had lost it. Med-bays that could reliably regrow an eye were few and far between.

I sent Spy a vision of her shoving all the weapons off the roof. I heard a little chuffing sound, and a semiautomatic landed in the dirt with a soft thud. A fully automatic weapon followed. I flinched as it fell, expecting it to fire. It didn't. More weapons joined them.

"Put it down, Marty," I said when everything went quiet. Marty bent to the ground, placed his weapon at his feet, and kicked it over to me.

"Who told you my name?" I asked.

Over comms, Mateo cursed softly, putting it together. He hadn't caught Marty's mistake.

Marty's face twitched just a hair. "I've always known your name."

I walked closer and leaned to him, sniffing, wondering if I could smell his fear. "Until today you knew me as Ms. Smith. That's all you've ever known me as. But a bit ago you called me"—I took a slow breath, my nose at his throat—"*Shining*." His pulse pounded in his neck. The sweat stink in his clothes was potent. "Tell me about Clarisse Warhammer."

He couldn't help his intake of breath. My skin caught a faint vibration of foreign nanobots in his sweat. That was interesting. I hadn't known I could detect them that way.

"Did Warhammer come by, looking for me? Ask you some questions?" He didn't react. "Did..." I stopped so close I could feel the damp heat of his body. "Did you get an offer to capture my friend, Harlan, and send him to her?"

Marty flinched. Mateo's cursing stopped. Jagger targeted Wanda's head. She whimpered.

Marty's eyes dilated and then constricted. Softly, so softly I wasn't sure he'd hear me, I asked, "Did you give Harlan to Warhammer? Did you help her kill my friend?" My tone dropped lower. "Maybe give her my address? Send her after me?"

"She. Shesheshe—" He stopped suddenly, only now realizing how deep this pit of trouble was. Really, *really* bad trouble. He licked his desert-dry lips. "She came by. Asked some questions. She—" he stopped again. "Ms. Smith, I didn't mean for anyone to get hurt. I liked Harlan. She told me she just wanted to talk to him."

"And you believed her," I stated, my quiet tone mocking.

Wanda spoke up. "She showed up here a few months back. Marty knew what she wanted and what she planned. You let me go and I'll tell you everything I know."

"And everything Marty knows?" Jagger asked.

"Yes," she said. "I know everything he does."

I smiled at Marty. Aimed at his gut. Pressed the blaster's trigger. He stood there, uncertainty on his face, followed by confusion. He looked down at the weapon. Frowned hard. Coughed softly. Blood boiled from his nose and trickled from his mouth. Marty fell at my feet. Twitched. Died.

"You killed my friend," I said to his corpse.

Killing Marty wasn't enough. Nothing would ever be enough.

I aimed another blast at his head until brains bubbled out his ears.

"Asshole, you and Amos bring the men down, truss them so they can breathe a little. Put the living and this piece of crap inside. Wanda and I are going to have a little chat." I walked over and took her from Jagger, shoving her against the door to the storefront. I searched her thoroughly and not at all gently, opened the door, and thrust her inside. She landed face down on the cool floor. I hauled her up with one fist and rammed her into a chair.

"You said you'd let me go," she said.

"I didn't say you'd have all your teeth."

Marty's keys in my pocket, I sat at the table where we had eaten a meal together, as the air conditioner cooled me. I sipped Marty's good coffee in the silence, and watched as his body began to cool and grow stiff on the floor at my feet, his bladder and bowels loosening. The two men who had been ready to kill me from the roof were sitting close by the body. They squirmed and worried, hands secured behind their backs, a rope pulling their arms so high that struggling meant pulling their shoulders out of joint. Their expressions said they knew they were in deep trouble and had no easy way out of the mess they were in. They weren't gagged, but neither of them spoke, their breaths panting, growing faster each time a cat curled up on them and rolled over on their crotches, looking up at them, showing teeth, hissing softly.

I thought it was funny, but I was beginning to think I might be slightly warped.

As I drank my coffee, Jagger and Cupcake secured the premises. Amos kept an eye on the two captives. Wanda, Marty's right-hand man, watched me. Eventually, I turned emotionless eyes to her. Into the quiet, I said, "Talk."

"A few months past—I have the date on the calendar if you need it—a woman calling herself Clarisse Warhammer showed up asking questions. She asked about Harlan and about crazy stuff, like spaceships and war weapons. She flashed around a *lot* of money and brought a camo-painted container for trade."

"Was she alone?"

"Two men, one with an eyepatch, but she was in charge. The three of them were still here when I went home for the day and were here when I came back the next day. He never said, but I know Marty. He slept with her and told her everything she wanted to know. The next time Harlan came by to do business, Marty coldcocked him, put him in a cage, and called Warhammer for a pickup. When she got here, the negotiations were totally private. I wasn't part of them. But Warhammer brought in the rest of the camo-painted containers when she picked up Harlan."

I poured more coffee. The trickle of liquid was loud in the silence. The cold air blowing up my back felt like heaven. Still quietly, I asked, "And you didn't call the Law about a man sold like a piece of meat?"

"What would I say?" she asked bitterly. "The Law loves Marty. If I called the cops and Marty handed them a wad of cash and sent them on their way? Then what? I'm out a job and Marty has me killed and my kid gets sent to the city orphanage." She went silent, watching me. Standing her ground. I found myself liking her. I wondered if Clarisse had touched her too.

I sipped and waited, letting the tension rise, my odd eyes on Wanda.

"I'll get those papers." She went to the computer and the file cabinet behind the desk. Amos maneuvered to cover her, a shotgun over the lip of the counter. He didn't look smart, but he was. I was liking Amos a lot too. I had a feeling that my nanobots would like anyone I could control, and that was a bad thing.

Wanda searched for and printed out all the business and personal paperwork Marty kept on premises.

She wrote a valid sales receipt to me, stating that the camo containers (specifying each one by number and location) and all the equipment in them were duly paid for by Smith's Junk and Scrap. Yesterday. "It's the least you deserve," she said.

I didn't reply.

It was blood money. Harlan's blood money.

Wanda placed all my paperwork as well as Warhammer's paperwork on the table by my coffee saucer. I looked at the small stack of papers. Then back up at her. She quailed just a little. Without comment, I flipped through the pages, spotted a few of Clarisse's that might prove interesting, folded the stack one-handed, and shoved it in a jeans pocket. I'd use the weapons in the containers—weapons that had paid for Harlan's death—to take Clarisse down.

Jagger made some calls and Marconi arranged for diesel rigs to haul away my containers. Cupcake and Jagger oversaw everything.

Wanda watched us for a while, and as the afternoon hours passed, she began to bring me more trade goods. The good stuff. The expensive stuff. I added them to the clinking bag. She told me everything she thought I might want to know and a lot that I had no interest in but might come in handy later. When she was done, I had gobs of info—one particular item invaluable. I stood, removed my gloves, and bent over the guards, holding my bare hands close to their faces. I felt no vibrations from Warhammer's nanobots. I re-gloved.

I stood and turned to Wanda, asking, "Did Clarisse Warhammer wear gloves?"

"Yes. Well, the first day. She wasn't wearing them when I came back the morning after."

"Did you get sick after she left?"

"Yes. Marty and I both had fevers. . . ." She stopped and stared at *my* gloved hands. "Did she have the . . . the Zombie plague? Am I going to break out in boils in a few weeks and go crazy?"

Everyone still alive remembered the plagues, especially the Zombie plague, transmitted by touch. The virus had come from the melting icecaps and had affected humans' brains.

"Do you have access to a med-bay?"

"Yes," she whispered, confusion on her face. "A portable one. It's in back."

"How are you getting home?"

"I have an old electric truck. Long bed."

I removed my gloves again and held out my bare sweaty hands. Wanda shrank back. I reached as if to touch her and felt the telltale vibration. "I'm sorry. She infected you. I feel it in your skin. I survived what Warhammer has and I have the . . . let's call them antibodies. I can share them with you. Then we can put the med-bay in the bed of your truck. When you go home, make arrangements for your kid for a week. You'll be sick again soon. Set the med-bay to monitor your vitals and flush you with fluids. Insert every Berger chip you can find to help your brain stay active. In seventy-two hours, you'll know if you live or die."

She cursed, still staring at my bare hands, then at the door, which was too far away. Big globular tears ran down her face. With no way out, Wanda placed her shaking hands in mine. They were cold.

I was ashamed that I felt nothing other than that. I pushed my mutated, altered nanobots, feeling them crawl across her skin, searching for entrance—any minuscule cut, abrasion, torn cuticle—and claimed her as mine. I gave it twenty minutes. When I was done, I sat down and pulled my gloves back on. I wasn't sure if a second transition was kinder than the actual Zombie plague or not.

"In sixty minutes, you can wash your hands. Not until then."

She took a frightened breath through parted lips.

"When we're done, you will get in your vehicle and go home. And stay there. You quit your job today because you got sick this morning and because your boss was selling black-market weapons. That will be your story. Where is Marty's safe?"

Wanda paled. She had carefully not mentioned a safe. She had planned on keeping the cash for herself. Not that I blamed her. "Half the cash in it is yours," I said. "But you have to lie low. And if you give me up to anyone, you'll go like Marty did." I looked at him and his henchmen, trying to decide what to do with them. Fortunately, before I thought it all through, Jagger came in. "I'd rather not have to dispose of them," I said to him, pointing at the prisoners. "Will Marconi take care of it?"

"Yeah. But it won't be pretty."

"No!" one of the men said. "Not Marconi."

"He'll give us to Mina," the other one said. "We'll do anything."

I sighed. I couldn't take them. Or better to say that I wouldn't. No matter how much my nanobots wanted to create a nest. To Jagger I said, "If they swear to McQuestion?"

"Doable. Better than being dead."

The prisoners looked at each other. Simultaneously they said, "Whatever that is, yes."

I said to Jagger, "Do it."

Jagger pulled his cell and stepped outside. Big rigs arrived, and Marty's container-moving equipment—a monster portable antigravity device—went to work lifting the containers and putting them on Marconi's truck beds.

After Wanda left for the last time, I sat in my chair, gloves on, sipping my third mug of coffee, and watched as Jagger handed over the two henchmen to a biker wearing an OMW kutte. Sat as they were hauled away in a new electric car. Sat as the camo-painted containers were hauled off and stored at the hotel until I could get them back to Smith's. I'd owe Marconi for this. Maybe he could take over Marty's scrapyard.

I stared at Marty on the floor and sipped some more. He was wearing khakis and a blue shirt. His belt matched his shoes. His shit stank. I had a feeling Marty would have been surprised at that.

I hated killing people. I hated the odd look in their eyes when they knew they were dead, that moment of surprise and uncertainty and shock when the pain hit and their blood boiled and their organs sizzled. But this guy? He killed Harlan as surely as if he tortured my friend himself. And Wanda had been right. If she called the Law, her future would have been even more doubtful and . . . fraught, maybe? . . . than the future she faced now. The Law was uncertain. Vengeance wasn't.

The sun threw long shadows. Cupcake entered, Jagger behind her, bringing with them the tantalizing smell of food. I hadn't eaten since breakfast. Spy slithered in with them and jumped to the office counter. Cupcake arranged hemp-based take-out containers in the center of the table and set out three fancy plates and silver utensils from Marty's stock. It was comfort food—eggs sunny-side up on top of fried wheat bread, with a platter of hash browns and a sliced tomato. And a bowl of grits with butter melted on top. Grits looked nasty.

Cupcake poured more coffee, which I didn't drink. Even with my nanobots, the caffeine had me shaking. They sat and we ate, as if there weren't a dead body stinking of feces and sour urine on the floor only feet away. I pushed away the grits and Jagger took them. The Mobile boy liked his Southern food, it seemed. I ate. And I ate. We all did. We didn't talk, which was good. I had no idea what to say.

When we were done, Cupcake brought out a garbage bag and dumped our debris into it, tying it and placing it near the door. She retook her seat. She stared at me. So did Jagger. I sighed. "Okay. Ask your questions."

"Warhammer created a nest, deliberately infecting people," Jagger said. "Tying them to her, using them for whatever she wanted. Why did *you* transition Wanda?"

"I didn't have a choice. Warhammer touched things in here, leaving her sweat everywhere. That left her nanobots behind. By accident, or on purpose, I don't know. Wanda had already transitioned. The boys you sent to McQuestion hadn't. If I left her like she was, Warhammer would eventually call her. Wanda would tell her about everything that happened here. And"—I looked at my gloved hands—"when we did attack Warhammer, Wanda would have died with her queen. I like Wanda."

"So far as we can tell," Cupcake said, "you only infected Mateo, us two, and now Wanda, which I understand. But what are you going to do with her?"

I looked at Jagger. "You stayed away. She can stay away too."

Jagger frowned, his whole face pulling down like a death mask. His voice was rough as sandpaper and his words bitter as wormwood when he rasped out, "I wake up wanting you. I want you every single moment of every single day. I spend every one of those moments trying to figure out how to please you. What you might need that I can provide or do to make sure you're safe and happy."

I went still as stone. Remembering the very few others I had touched in my life.

"The nights are worse. I wake up in the night, thrashing from dreams"—he took a breath that sounded pained—"wanting you. I fight the need to come to you every single day. Wanda will not be able to fight the compulsion to come to you. It might not be bad for the first few weeks, but she'll come looking for you out of desperation."

Spy jumped on the table and brought her nose to my face. It wasn't a *talk to me* gesture. It was pure cat, scenting me. "Did you feed the cats?" I asked Cupcake.

"Marty had some cooked shrimp in the fridge. They smelled a little off, but the cats liked them fine."

Spy sprawled across the table. Two other cats joined her from somewhere, sniffing and curious, before stretching out and beginning the job of grooming. I rubbed my scalp and turned back to Jagger. "I thought the Berger-chip programs were helping you."

"They do," Jagger replied. "But nothing makes the need for you go away."

"That compulsion is one major reason why I don't transition people, that and the dying part. The first ones I transitioned died. It was horrible."

I had accidently transitioned a young biker I liked by touching his hand in passing. He got sick and died. And I deliberately transitioned Pops in the vain attempt to keep him alive when he was dying horribly. I hadn't known what I was doing. He died too. And then I found Mateo, a slave of the sheriff in a nearby town, also dying, because mech nanobots from a battle with a space-worthy PRC Mama-Bot had gotten inside his warbot suit and were eating him alive. He had been badly injured, but he had figured out how to kill the mech nanobots in and on equipment. At his direction, I put his suit under Smith's big AG Grabber to decontam, and him in the med-bay for palliative treatment since there was no cure. Humans didn't survive under WIMP antigravity energies.

But he kept fighting. Kept trying to live.

The mech-nanos infecting him were so numerous that my only option was to transition him to my own bio-mech-nanos, hoping they would be able to convert the PRC nanos and repair some of the damage. It took weeks, and I monitored him every second. I flushed so much fluid through his system that Mateo should have drowned. Yet he survived. Because he was brain damaged, I uploaded him with Berger chips to reteach him everything.

He developed autonomy of a sort. My first success.

And then the man from Naoma who wanted to date me. He had touched my things in my office. That was when I learned the nanobots in my sweat and blood lived for a while on things I touched. He got sick, and I kept him alive using med-bay protocols I had created for Mateo, but without the Berger chips. He survived.

But he got persistent, repeatedly showing up at the scrapyard, begging me to be his girlfriend, his wife, his anything. He followed me. Stalkerish. When he attacked me, Mateo killed him and put his body under some scrap. I guessed his bones were still there.

Now I had Mateo, Jagger, Cupcake, and Wanda, who had a kid. Jagger was right. She would show up at some point, and I would have to take her in. I was building a nest whether I wanted one or not.

"Bloody hell," I whispered. "Bloody damn hell."

"Why do you say that?" Cupcake asked. "Why not *shit* or *fuck* like normal people?"

I grinned slightly. "The first time I said *shit*, Pops backhanded me across the room. He gave me a list of appropriate cuss words, and *shit* and *fuck* were not on it. I liked the ones he used, so *bloody damn* and *hell* and *bugger* it is." I thought a moment. "Sometimes *bollocks*."

"Wanda?" Jagger asked, returning us to the problems at hand.

My smile fell away. "All I can do is wish her good luck."

Jagger crossed his big arms and said, "Eventually McQuestion's going to find out about you being Shining Smith. What do I tell him?"

"Why should anyone find out—?" I stopped. Clarisse Warhammer was telling people who I was. The MS Angels had to know. McQuestion would learn through his network of spies. The reappearance of Shining Smith would hit the rank and file of the Outlaws like a wrecking ball, which I had been trying to avoid for so many years. And he would ask Jagger about me. Jagger knew I was Shining Smith. Jagger was keeping secrets from his boss. No OMW was permitted divided loyalties. That was a death sentence.

The false memories had held for a while. And then I had kissed him, reinoculating him. He was mine. He'd never betray me. He mentally, physically, and emotionally couldn't. He'd die first.

I could have come to care for Jagger, except I'd never know if he liked me for me or because his brain had been rewired. He was still loyal to McQuestion, but only in situations where the two loyalties didn't clash. Jagger was in deadly danger.

"Tell him who you think I am. Bring him for a visit, and we'll deal." I checked my chrono. "We have eight hours of night left, ten before full light. We going after the Simba?"

"Yeah," Jagger said. "One problem. According to Marconi, there's a local gang camping near it. They have a rep as bad as the old MS-13. And they have weapons. Lots of weapons. When the Law tried to go after them, Marconi says they kidnapped a cop's wife and sent her home in pieces. The Law's done nothing to stop them since."

"Will the Law object to us going after them?"

"Not a lick. They might even cheer us on."

"Okay. Let's get out of here." I looked around. "Poor Marty died in a terrible fire."

"Got it," Jagger said.

I frowned. "Did Marty have family?"

"A grown daughter somewhere. Wife died in the war. A girlfriend who dances in the Pink Bunny Gentleman's Club," Cupcake said.

I glanced at her. "Make sure they each get something in the mail. Anonymously."

"Will do," she said.

I left the building, turning my back on Marty on the floor. If local officials did a proper postmortem, they would know he had been dead for hours before he burned, but I was betting on the city not having a proper forensics med-bay. And not wanting to spend the money on a dodgy character.

With Marty gone, I'd have to rebuild all my contacts in this city, not something Jagger could do. But once Clarisse was dead, maybe it was something Wanda could do. If she had a job to serve me, that might keep her away from me. I wrapped a fist around the grab handle and swung into the diesel cab's passenger seat, almost landing on Spy in my chair. She gave it up with ill grace. "Don't you give me that look," I said to her. "Now I'll have your cat hair all over my butt." She sniffed at me and jumped onto the dash.

Amos climbed into the back of the bed, which was loaded with I-had-no-idea-what, beyond the Antigravity Grabber, except he had claimed a recliner from somewhere and strapped it in. He stretched out the footrest as he got comfy, guns in his lap.

Cupcake placed Marty's food and water supplies in with our growing stash of confiscated items, climbed into the cab, and started the diesel, the thrum a cat call, literally. They came from everywhere. Leaping and running and stinking of rat. Spy slithered into my lap, curled up, and closed her eyes. It took maybe two seconds and she was purring.

Barely avoiding jackknifing, Cupcake wheeled us around and out of Marty's. As we pulled away, I watched the view in the overlarge side mirror, and saw the burst of flame as it shot out the open door of the storefront. The entire building was in flames in moments. Against the glare of fire, I saw Jagger silhouetted in black as he and his bike pulled out behind us.

As we drove, I went through Marty's shipping manifests and discovered that one of my new containers, 374, was dedicated to brand-new armored suits. I wasn't acquisitive by nature, believing that all things were to be bartered away if the price was right, but . . . *armor*. Brand-new *military* armor. *Oh, yeah.* My covetous heart wanted armor. My armor at home had been top-of-the-line space armor before the end of the war. It was excellent, but it was a decade from new and not designed with explosive weapons, atmosphere, and full gravity in mind. If the manifest was right, these would be better.

We dropped off the unnecessary gear at the hotel and showered again. My mutated nanos lived only a few minutes in water, and seventy-two hours on dry surfaces, so being clean was vital. Plus, any excuse for a water shower. Out back, in the overflow-parking security area, I found container number 374 at the back of the lot, hidden from prying eyes by the other containers, and used Marty's special key to open the lock. The high-tech lock made a tiny whirring sound as it released. "Oh, yeah. Come to mama," I whispered.

I pulled on the door, and it rammed outward against me, loud noises banging inside. Only Jagger's quick reflexes saved me; he was instantly there, his bigger body mass holding the door open only a crack as things slammed against the inside. His arms were over me, bracing the door, making a cage of protection around my body. He smelled like sweat and woodsy cologne, sandalwood maybe.

"Thanks," I said, suddenly breathless, trying not to respond to his straining body, his chest an inch from me, his arms quivering with stress, and that amazing scent. I pulled a flashlight and shined it into the crack. Boxes stamped with Uncle Sam's seal and *MAII 2050*. Military armor for sure. Box after box. I swept the inside with the light.

Each armor suit had its own box, and the 12-meter container was stuffed full. The boxed suits had shifted during transport. I slipped out from under Jagger, though being under him sounded pretty wonderful right now.

"It's like a rockslide in there. Let it go, but jump back. And by the way. It's all armor."

"All of it?" he asked.

I grinned at him in the darkness. "Chock-full."

"Little Girl, I like your luck today." He gave me a devil-may-care flash of teeth in his scruffy late-night beard, and sprang away. The door banged open, boxes tumbling to the ground until the pile below was tall enough to stop the rockslide. Box-slide.

As if the universe was my buddy again, I spotted a suit for a female body type, adjustable between 1.5 meters and 1.8 meters and 45 to 90 kilos. It would fit me. The label said it was automated, actively repositioning Dragon Scale exoskeleton armor with anti-recoil sleeves and legs, heat and cold resolution, Chameleon-skin visual shielding, and was formatted with fourteen different enviro camouflage patterns.

I might have made a cooing sound as I dragged it to the side, tore open the box, and pulled the suit out of its molded hemp-plaz packing. I held it up to me. It was a peculiar matte gray that seemed both iridescent and full of shadows, like a black pearl at sunset. The scales overlapped like snake scales, almost organic in the way they moved when I bent a sleeve. "You are so pretty," I whispered to the suit. I wanted to be in it, but the box was otherwise empty, no donning chamber within.

Before I could ask, Jagger called out from inside the container, "There's a bigger box at the back. Looks like a portable donning station." Jagger shoved the bigger box across the tumbled boxes, and it landed with a *whomp* and a puff of dust. Jagger dropped down beside it and tore it open. The donning device was stacked in easy-to-assemble sections, could armor up to eight people at one time, and came with a Berger plug-in to walk him through the setup. I was beginning to think the military had gotten this one right. The donning station assembly was idiot-proof. Just in time, Cupcake and Amos showed up to help, and the cats helped by getting in the way. Despite the cats, the station went together, forming an eight-sided circle.

An octagon, my Berger chip started. I touched it off.

The donning station's power source was in the middle, the stations facing out. Its batteries showed green, and it powered up fast with a nearly painful hum of electronics, casting long shadows and flickering lights in red, green, and blue across the secure parking area.

Each of the eight narrow niches was numbered—one through eight. They had stubby arms that stuck out straight, a neck rest, and a crotch wedge for rough measurements. I lifted my armor suit and held it to the back of number one. Nothing happened. After a moment, I looked over my shoulder at Jagger, who was listening to the Berger plug-in and said, "Try tapping the pads there with both index fingers to initialize." He pointed near the suit's hands. I pressed the tiny bumps, and, with a soft sucking whoosh, the armor was yanked away from me, molding to the back of the donning unit. It opened with multiple clicks, like a lobster shell cracking open, the interior a shimmery silver that was hard to focus on.

Jagger, Cupcake, and Amos placed their suits into niches two through four. The donning station clicked, whooshed, and they snapped into place too. Amos walked around the entire system and stopped in front of unit number four and the shimmering, open, outsized suit there. "I'mma be bad*ass* in this shit."

I stripped down to undies and tank top and stepped onto the low mounting pedestal, my feet centered in the outline. Turning my back to the armor suit in the same way I did at the scrapyard with the armor I'd taken from the *SunStar*, I sucked in a deep breath, held it, and began a mental countdown. I closed my eyes and my mouth loosely, forced my muscles to relax, and held utterly motionless, hands down and out to my sides. I began to blow out the breath. "Initiating auto-donning," a tinny voice said, coming from near my ear.

The armor positioning arm slid out and encircled my waist, snugging me into the torso segment. The armor sections began snapping over my body, interlocking, shrinking, and expanding to my exact measurements, repositioning against muscles and joints, expanding and contracting to fit me. Snugging tight. I fought the desire to bolt as the helmet and face piece locked over me.

Claustrophobia and memories from my own piece of hell stabbed into me like knives. The respiratory tube shoved between my lips, into my mouth, and against my cheek with a puff of stale air. I exhaled that first puff, inhaled slowly on the second. The armored boots snapped shut midcalf.

I stretched out my fingers, knowing the worst was still to come, and forced myself to hold utterly still. I breathed. Again. Again. The glove sectionals encasing my fingers slid and shifted to the proper lengths.

"Prepare for peripheral nerve engagement, left hand," the speaker said. I gasped and swore as minuscule needles, thinner and finer than acupuncture needles, pierced my palms, along the sides of my fingers, and into my fingertips. "Bloody damn," I spat. The pain was like having my hand set on fire. "Prepare for peripheral nerve engagement, right hand." It too engaged. Sharp, burning, cutting, and then intensely icy as the chemicals coating the needles in my hands began to take the pain away. The worst was over.

I opened my eyes, looking out into the night through the suit's visual screen and sensors—some low-light sensors that let me see clear as day, some infrared, and some high-tech, designed to break through known heat and cold shielding. Fancy electronics, way better than my old suit.

"Do you wish catheter and bowel removal collection to be initiated at this time?"

"No. God no." Once, long ago, the first time I tried on armor, I had made the mistake of saying yes. Never again. I'd pee in the suit and let it slosh in my boots first.

"Liquid oxygen breathing supply required?" the speaker asked.

I said into the tiny speaker inside the faceplate, "No. Current Earth atmosphere, night desert conditions, West Virginia."

"Complying," the suit said. "Except for critical chest and head areas, this suit is a soft suit until hard suits are required. Should environmental factors or physical attack necessitate suit hardening, a tone will sound." I heard a soft tone. "This indicates that Dragon Scale hardening is imminent. If wearer wishes to negate suit hardening, wearer must say either, 'Postpone,' or 'Reject.' Otherwise, Dragon Scales will convert. This will take approximately one second, during which the suit will not move."

"Lack of movement while under attack?" I asked.

"Correct. All suit-monitoring sensors are on the upper left screen. This suit should be charged to full capacity before using. The suit is currently at forty-six percent power. This provides approximately twenty-two hours of normal, non-combat usage. Full combat usage will drain this suit's current power levels to zero in less than seven hours.

"All others of your unit may be located and followed via screen number two at the lower left. Other sensors and screens may be positioned by use of the buttons on the left palm."

I stepped down the small rise to the pavement, my combat boots silent and comfortable as jogging shoes. The night was completely alive; I could see as well as in daylight, though the color palate was gray, green, and glittering silver. And I could see what was behind me. There were no blind spots. I held out my arms, and the scales covering my arms and legs interlocked and shifted with every movement. This suit was *bloody brilliant*!

Cupcake was a yellow glow to my left in the unit-member screen. Jagger was blue. Amos was pink and shaped like a big teddy bear, which I did not tell him. We locked up the armor container and geared up from another container of goodies, choosing weapons for the fight with the gang, and tools to free the Simba. We used the anti-recoil feature in reverse, to toss heavy equipment around and lock everything up. It was going to be a very long, tiring night. But I did so love new toys.

We left the parking area secure, under the control of two of Jagger's people—Outlaws by their garb, totally loyal to him by their attitude. OMW riders in Hell's Angels' territory was a recipe for disaster. We needed to get out of here fast, before Marconi got wind of Jagger's people.

Cupcake drove the rig, headlights bouncing in the darkness, Jagger and Amos in the back (which was now empty except for its passengers, a huge pump, and an Antigravity Grabber). I sat shotgun, and the cats took over the dash, tails twitching with excitement.

We picked up the earth movers, which was a lot easier than I expected thanks to my new AG Grabber. The rig was carrying far more than its approved weight capacity, but we crossed the river and turned upstream at a steady six kilometers an hour. I could walk faster than that, but with the weight and the condition of the roads, I couldn't complain.

Impatient, I tapped my comms. "You there?"

"Copy," Mateo said. His voice changed slightly, sounding almost gentle, a tone I rarely heard. "You've done amazingly well."

A glow rushed through me. Praise had come seldom in my life. "Thanks."

"Are you okay after Marty?"

The question hit me in the gut like an icy sucker punch, and the glow vanished. I wasn't thinking about Marty, neither his betrayal nor his death. "No. But I'll deal with it when I get home."

"Copy that." He went silent. Mateo understood nightmares.

To keep from seeing the look in Marty's eyes as he died, I tapped comms to Jagger. "You get confirmation from Marconi that we can take out the gang operating in his region?"

"His exact words were, 'You do this for my city, and I will open peace and territory negotiations with McQuestion.' And he's keeping the Law occupied elsewhere tonight."

"He's not going to start a riot, is he?"

"We agreed that collateral damage was foolish. Otherwise he's in full control."

"I'm going to regret this, aren't I?"

Jagger sighed softly, "I regret everything since I met you, Little Girl."

And just like that, Jagger broke my heart.

Two hours later, we made a slow left into the trees and came to a stop, the engine rumbling. It was blacker than the lowest pit of hell when I opened the door and the cats bounded out, vanishing, exploring. I swung out of the cab, shut the door, and Cupcake locked the truck armor into place. I caught a glimpse of Amos and Jagger as they disappeared into the trees on the other side of the narrow two-rut road. I gave Cupcake a thumbs-up, dropped low, and crab-walked into the brush, where I slid my battle faceplate into place and actuated temperature shielding and low-light-sensor blocking software on the Chameleon skin. I initiated the anti-recoil in the Dragon Scale's arms and legs. And I went ahead and requested hardening of the armor. And *bloody hell* that *hurt*! The suit went from comfy and stretchy to what felt like wearing a full-body steel corset in one second.

Cupcake began a slow crawl along the road, the diesel engine loud enough to wake the dead—or a drugged, drunken, and sleeping gang. Moving fast, thanks to my nanobot modifications, I preceded the cab's bouncing lights.

I had a long-range RADR blaster and old-fashioned ARGO gas-operated shotgun secured at my spine, a powerful short-range blaster on my left thigh beside a wicked blade, two ten-millimeter semiautomatic handguns—one on my right thigh, one at my back—and what Pops called an "I'm fucked" weapon at one ankle, for when everything was lost and I needed to shoot myself to avoid capture. I didn't need holsters. The armor came with little foldouts that formed locking mechanisms to hold my gear, including the bag of extra magazines above my left buttock.

Just ahead, I saw campfires, cars parked or abandoned here and there, tents and RVs. No sentries. No detectable sensors. I raced in from tree to tree, and then from rusted hulk to RV.

Dogs were chained to trees, sleeping, curled into tight balls of despair.

Music boomed through speakers—something with a cello, postwar and disjointed, as if the cello had been shot full of holes—loud enough to hide the diesel roar. I circled on the edge of the campsite, my suit sensors still spotting no cameras, no lasers, no warning systems.

There was a small cage to one side, and it was full of people. Standing room only, crammed too full to allow anyone to lie down. The stench was horrible, and I initiated air filters as I one-armed myself up into a tree and raced along a branch over the cage. Prisoners. Emaciated. Naked. Bleeding. Women and children and what had once been pretty boys. A memory of the woman in the log house flashed through my mind. Was there a connection? If so, what?

"Let's make them pay," I whispered into my mic.

"Approaching from the south," Jagger said. "Prisoners are in the furthest RV."

Amos said, "I just brained a guy taking a piss. There's a handcuffed woman in his tent."

"We have to assume that every tent and RV has prisoners in them," I said. "We'll have to clear each one. No quarter given to anyone who"—I took a slow breath to control my anger—"hurt prisoners."

"Roger that," Jagger murmured.

Amos said, "I hope these suits kill bedbugs and lice. 'Cause *dayum* this place stinks."

"I have visual on the campsite," Cupcake said.

"I see two speakers," I said. "When the diesel is close, kill the speakers so they can hear the engine. When they come running out, everyone with a weapon dies. Everyone else will be treated humanely until we discover who decided not to be human and not to act human. When we leave here, there will be no more bad guys."

"Roger that," Jagger repeated, his voice the battlefield ice of the warrior who survived the Battle of Mobile. "Targeting speakers."

"What he said," Amos said.

I stretched out along the branch and pulled the ancient ARGO. It could accept extra-large-capacity mags, holding fifteen rounds each, and I had four more mags in my butt bag. I dragged the bag forward and positioned it for easy retrieval. I located each of my fellow warriors in the face-shield sensors and checked their firing positions. So far, so good. Shooting each other by accident should be difficult.

The diesel cab bumped over ruts. Cupcake shifted gears. "Now," she said.

Shots rang out. The music died. The engine roared. The truck bounced into the main camp area, the horn blowing like the coming of the Angel Gabriel. I initiated my ear protectors. Men stumbled out of RVs, out of tents, rubbing eyes, drunk, all armed. They started firing at the cab. I took down the one nearest me. Then another. And another. From the sides, Jagger and Amos took down two more.

The armed men scattered like ants, each positioned in my sensor screens. Each obviously thinking that the shooting came from the diesel, they took cover from it, leaving themselves fully exposed to us. I shot two in the back. OMW rules of engagement meant killing people, not etiquette.

With our armor shielding and the glaring lights from the big rig, they couldn't see us. I emptied my magazine one careful shot at a time, changed mags, and scanned the battleground. I went around again, putting a second shot into each of the downed men. Just in case. It was like shooting rats in a bucket.

When the last one was down and the shooting stopped, I said, "Kill the engine, Cupcake." The diesel died with a slow coughing rumble. The ear protectors that had covered my ears during the barrage allowed ambient sounds in again. People were screaming and weeping.

I shoved back my faceplate and swung down, landing in front of the cage. A woman stared at me with wide blank eyes. The cage wire had pressed diamond patterns into her face and abdomen where she had been asleep standing up. I swung the ARGO shotgun back, and the suit grabbed it, holding it secure. Soundless, the woman watched as I inspected the cage's lock. It was an old steel padlock, operated with a key. The lock was well built, but the hasp latch was cheap metal.

"Dick has the key," she whispered, her voice a rasp.

I wrapped my armored hand around the padlock and pulled, twisting. The metal groaned. I placed one foot on the cage wall and activated the recoil-reverse feature of the armor. I pulled harder. The suit adjusted and hardened to provide maximum force and torque. My glove went harder than steel. I twisted my hand slightly.

The latch snapped off. I yanked the door open. People spilled from the cage into a pile on the ground, too exhausted to catch their balance or stand upright. The stench was appalling.

Gunshots rang out.

I didn't even bother to turn around. My screens showed that Amos and Jagger had both fired, taking down someone. "Secure the area," I said over comms. "Call in Medic."

"Hand of the Law and Medic are busy in town with Marconi's diversion," Jagger said.

"*Bloody hell*. So we're on our own." I leaned down and helped people up until I found the woman who had spoken to me earlier. I offered her my hand.

Her breath caught when she moved. "Broken ribs," she said, matter-of-fact, as she stood.

"Do you know where the medical supplies are stored?" I asked. "Water? Food?"

"Yes." She lifted a hand as if to point, but her fingers were swollen and twisted, broken and left to heal out of shape. They looked as if she had tried to set the bones herself. "In that RV."

"Do they have a med-bay?"

"Yes. Rudimentary. A first-generation MBB. For

battle triage and stabilization only." That was medical and soldier jargon. When I looked at her, she said, "I was a nurse. My name's Gretchen."

"No. You *are* a nurse. Those men? They did *not* take away who you are."

Her eyes passed through a series of changes as the words settled into some wounded place inside her. Tears gathered at the corners of her eyes and instantly dried. She looked away.

I carefully didn't touch her. "Hey. See that woman?" I pointed to Cupcake who was striding through the carnage with a tread that radiated rage. She passed a downed man, and when he twitched, she pulled a weapon, shot him in the head, and reholstered so fast the motion was nearly invisible. I was so proud of her. She stopped and picked up something from the ground near her target. I tapped my comms to include her. "Her name is Cupcake. She can do anything, *anything,* that needs doing. You two get things organized—med-bay, water, and food. Make sure the children are cared for."

Cupcake stopped in front of me. "Gretchen is a nurse," I said to her. "She knows where everything is."

Cupcake and Gretchen exchanged nods. Cupcake held open a long jacket she had picked up from the ground, standing back like a servant or a gentleman in an old film. Gretchen eased her broken hands into the sleeves and pulled the front together. Cupcake leaned forward slowly and offered flex ties. "I can secure the front," she said gently.

"Thank you," Gretchen whispered.

"Jagger," I said into comms, pointing. "Clear that RV. There's water and medical supplies in it."

"Roger that." He bounded up the steps. Shots rang out. Jagger returned fire once. Twice. Two bodies flew through the air and landed in a heap, moaning.

"Those men?" I nodded to the injured bad guys. "You can have them. Your kidnappers and abusers are yours to do with what you want."

Gretchen looked up at me and something fierce

crossed her face. "Good. But it will never be enough."

"Get your people organized," I repeated. "Get them help. We can call in the sheriff in the morning."

"Make sure it isn't Deputy Darson. He's a regular."

"Is he now? I wonder how that will go over with the officer whose wife died out here."

Gretchen's voice was emotionless when she said, "Who do you think killed her?"

I cursed and walked away, leaving her and Cupcake in charge. They began issuing orders, taking over medical care, and apportioning food and water. I shut down the chatter. I tried not to look at the former prisoners, but an idea sprang up and wriggled in the back of my brain like a worm on a hook. I looked at the dead men. Three were wearing washed-out night camo.

I told my suit to soften. It didn't. I tried a couple different words, and it was still battle hard.

Jagger was chuckling into my earbuds. "Try 'Pliable Mode.'"

I did, and the suit went back to pajama soft.

"Tents and RVs are cleared," he said. "Bringing three bad guys. Where do you want them?"

"Truss them to the big tree near the fire pit. Add any who are wounded but still alive. They belong to the women and children they hurt."

I felt Jagger's reaction roil through the nanobots that connected us. "Roger that," he said softly.

With security in place, Jagger and Amos disappeared into the brush, carrying equipment that would ping and locate the Simba—assuming that the information we had on the main battle tank's location had been accurate. Assuming the Simba was anything more than a bit of imagination, battle legend, and wishful thinking.

Twenty minutes later Jagger said, "I got a ping."

I found his location on my screen and hardened my suit. "Cupcake?"

"We got this," she said. "Three hours to dawn.

Go."

Carrying the AI Interface Portal—the uplink for the Simba—carefully in both hands, I trudged through the trees and found the men in an open area on the far side of a creek. Amos was hip-deep in mud, Jagger chest-deep, pulling himself out of the wetland muck, his suit on full battle power, the anti-recoil mechs doing the work.

To me, Amos said, "I'm standing on something flat, made of metal, with metal protrusions."

Jagger said, "The dimensions are perfect. It has to be the Simba, but it's in total lockdown. Amos and I think we can dig out the mud and get close enough to the top of the Simba to find the access hatch. Then we can sandbag around the hatch, clean it out, and open the uplink access."

"There has to be four feet of mud," I said quietly. "It'll take days."

"Evelyn doesn't have days," Mateo said over the comms.

Amos moved through the mud toward me. Tripped. Fell forward, landed face-first in unsealed armor in the mud. He came out of the mud with a bound of recoil and almost flew up into the air. When he landed on his feet, he was standing in only two feet of mud, and his face shield was sealed. Over comms, he said, "I fucking love this suit! Does the hatch stick up from the tank's main body? 'Cause I just scratched my new armor on something."

Jagger waded to him and sealed his faceplate. He disappeared beneath the mud, moving here and there, creating a wake in a four-meter square. He stood upright, slinging and dripping mud. "Hatch is right here."

"I'm your good-luck charm," Amos said, wading around as if searching for something else to trip over. He looked like a two-meter pinecone in the Dragon Scale armor.

"Time frame for Simba extraction?" I asked.

"Dawn," Jagger said.

"That puts us driving the Simba out of here in daylight, instead of under the cover of darkness." I shook my head. "We need to be twenty miles away by dawn."

"Got another hatch," Amos said. He was standing right in front of me, this time only buried to his ankles. "Can I keep this suit?"

Jagger dove into the mud again and came up fast. He pushed back his helmet and mud went flying. "No," he said to Amos, "but you can drive the earthmover."

"I'll make this mud my bitch," the man said.

In forty minutes, the rear hatch of the Simba had been sandbagged, pumped free of mud, washed out, repumped, and dried. Jagger was inflating a massive bladder that would divert the creek when they were finished uncovering the Simba. Amos was moving muck, chortling like a happy four-year-old as he ran the earthmover.

I slid into the muck, stepped over and into the ring of sandbags that protected the hatch—which looked a lot like the airlock hatches on the skin of the *SunStar*. I was hoping that the seals had held and the Simba wasn't full of mud and water. That would suck.

The night was blacker than the devil's heart, as Pops used to say, but in my armor's face shield, I could see clear as day. I ran my fingers all around the hatch, finding it smooth, solid, perfectly machined. I sat on one side of the hatch and shifted the Interface Portal uplink on my lap. Gingerly, I inserted the hard probe on the uplink into the matching slot at the hatch of the Simba. It fit on the first try. "Okay," I said to Mateo back at the scrapyard. "It's up to you and Jolene."

"We got this, sugah," Jolene said.

I was glad someone had something. Suddenly all I had was the shakes. Bad ones. In the darkness all around me, I could see Marty's face as he died, and Gretchen's eyes when she began to come back to life—her horror, her pain. I shoved back my face shield again. I sipped water. I waited. I told myself I didn't have to pee. Over the comms I heard whirrs and snaps and clicks and a steady hum of electronic chatter.

I stared at the stars overhead. Millions of stars in the dry air of the night sky. From beneath my butt on the hatch, I felt something vibrate.

I jumped away, landing hip-deep in mud, the surface beneath my battle boots slanted. Arms flailing, I caught my balance. Whipped around to the hatch. A deeper blackness cracked in the center of the ring of sandbags. "Mateo?" I whispered. "The hatch? It's opening."

"Once it's fully open, drop in and re-plug the uplink inside. The socket will be to the right of the hatch rings, glowing yellow. Once the hatch is completely open, you have twenty seconds before the hatch closes again and you'll be stuck until I can get there."

"What?!" I said. "I'll be stuck until you rescue me?"

"Twenty seconds is a lot of time. As soon as you complete the process, I'll take over and operate it from the junkyard."

There was something odd in his voice, a nervous pacing of words, something not normal. "Mateo—"

"Power levels are low, Shining. Three seconds before the hatch is fully open."

"I don't like it." But I followed instructions to the letter. I unplugged the IP and dropped inside the utter blackness. My body hung, seemingly weightless as I fell for over two meters. I landed, a hard jolt absorbed by the suit's anti-recoil. "*Bloody hell*," I grunted. Around me was nothing. Not a thing. It was that dark. My mind conjured skulls and Bug-aliens. My heart raced. *Twenty seconds.* I had twenty seconds. There was no glowing yellow ring.

I didn't know which buttons to initiate on the

glove, so I whispered "Flashlight, external" to the suit, and a beam came on, small and focused forward, from my chest. Directly into a wall of dead electronics. My left glove buzzed, a faint vibration, and I looked down to see indicator lights. The oxygen levels around me were acceptable, my heart rate was too fast, and I was below ground. Good to know. Beside the altimeter was a flashlight icon. I pressed the increase button and more beams came on. I turned in a circle. The hatch I had dropped into was the one for the warbot suit. It was huge.

"You okay?" Jagger asked, the faceplate and armor sensors allowing me to maintain contact with the others.

"No," I griped, spotting the socket. I jammed the IP plug into it. A keyboard lit up. Too slow, too faint. I manually keyed Mateo's code, saying, "Mateo, four, eight, one, six, alpha tango delta." Beside it was the faint outline of a five-fingered human hand. I gripped my right glove in my teeth and ripped it off. The pain was out the roof as the needles released, but I placed my bare palm on the hand plate.

As I did, the hatch closed. What now? Had Mateo lied to me about me having a safety net of twenty seconds? Had he stuck me here? Why?

A shudder ran across my body and tripped my racing heart. *"Bloodyhellbloodyhellbloodyhell,"* I chanted under my breath over and over. Seconds passed. I was still chanting when a faint vibration juddered up through the soles of my feet.

The Simba came alive, saying, "Suit Initiated Main Battle Armored Tank is active. Batteries are at redline five percent. This battle tank requires a minimum of twelve percent battery capacity to initiate sensors, and twenty-seven percent to be considered battleworthy."

"We're out of power," I said into my comms. I put my glove back on, which *hurt*, and looked around for something wet to decontam the hand plate.

"I got this." Vibrations from outside told me

Jagger was doing something. I had no idea what. But he could hear me. The discoverers of Entangled Dark Neutrinos were my new bestest friends. Clanks and thuds reached me through the skin of the super-armored tank. A heavy thump sounded through the hatch.

"Simba requires basic WIMP power or three days of solar gain power to extricate from current location," the tank said, talking to someone. Not me.

"That sucks," I murmured. *And I'm stuck.* But I didn't say that. Yet. I found a cloth in a tight little pocket on my suit and added water from the suit's water supply. I scrubbed the hand-plate clean of my sweat and nanobots.

"Okay. Got it. Shining, attempt to activate the airlock and get out of there," Jagger said.

Thinking that nothing in life was ever that easy, I unlocked my face shield and slid it out of the way. It telescoped closed at the back of my neck. I was in love with this suit.

The Simba's air was machine-sour and dank but bearable. I directed the suit lights above and grabbed a lever. Twisted it around. A brighter slit of darkness appeared around the edge of the hatch as it began to slowly open. *Bloody thing worked*! I engaged the reverse-recoil feature of my armor and leaped from the floor. Toward the opening hatch.

I banged the back of my head on the hatch rim as I jumped. Passed the sandbags and flew into the air.

I landed beside the hatch in a four-limb crouch, the anti-recoil feature of this suit too good to be true. Behind me, the hatch began to close.

And then I felt the pain. *Bad.* I yanked off my glove again and reached a hand to the back of my head. Something wet met my fingers. I held them to the suit lights.

I was bleeding.

I had left my nanobots inside the closed hatch.

"Mateo?" I whispered. "We got problems."

"Talk to your boyfriend somewhere else," Jagger

said. "I'm transferring power and I need this space."

Mateo said, "Specify problems."

"I said, *move*," Jagger snarled.

I had kissed him. Right. Things were happening inside him. In the lights of the suit, I stepped on top of the sandbags and jumped to the shore, stepping over hardwires that came from somewhere ahead in the dark.

"I banged my head on the hatch. I left blood behind."

Mateo cursed. It was fairly inventive for a cyborg with half a brain.

"Wash your head," Mateo said, after a too-long pause. "Jagger, the tank was infested with PRC mech-nanos. Clean that wound with strong antiseptic, *now*, and seal up the bloody cloths until you can get them under an AG."

Jagger landed beside me, picked me up, and raced back toward the clearing.

As Mateo's words settled inside me, everything came clear. "You sorry, bloody son of a bitch," I said. The Simba hadn't been accidently buried. No. It had been infested with PRC nanobots and deliberately buried.

Instead of nuking the Simba, someone in the military must have found a way to put the bots to sleep, so they'd stop deconstructing the tank, then had sealed the tank and buried it to keep it safe until scientists learned how to kill the little suckers. Mateo had discovered how to kill the PRC nanos all on his own. He had discovered the Simba and its history. He knew I, or someone I transitioned, could likely survive being infested with PRC nanobots during a rescue mission.

He had used me to get himself a war machine to rescue his . . . his what? Evelyn had been his second in command. They had probably been a lot more than that.

Mateo had sent me into the infected Simba to start it up. Had made sure we'd have an antigravity device big enough to power up the Simba and zap the nanobots on site. He now had the Simba, earthmovers to free it, and two portable Antigravity Grabbers. My *thrall* had done that. On his own.

"What have you done?" I whispered to Mateo.

"What I have to, to rescue Evelyn and kill the queen."

"You could have asked," I whispered.

"You never asked *me*," he said.

"You didn't have a brain to ask," I said.

I was infected all over again. My nanobots would have to fight the pure PRC mech-nanos I picked up in the Simba. Mine would probably win, but I'd need a med-bay in less than seventy-two hours.

Jagger opened the truck door, stepped up high, sat, and cradled me on his lap. When Gretchen tried to help, he accepted a wound kit and sent her on her way. "Gloves," I snapped. Jagger was already pulling on a pair over his armored hands. Gently, he cleaned my wound. "Don't touch your face," I said.

"Copy that," he said.

My heart thundered. I wanted to smash something. Mateo had . . . Mateo had betrayed me.

"I remember the moment I first saw you," Jagger murmured, "sitting there in that silly getup, grime under your nails. That awful orange nail polish chipped and dirty." He dabbed my wound, dropping bloody cloths into the empty wound kit. A lot of bloody cloths.

He pressed my scalp, trying to stanch the blood, the stuff on the cloths stinging like dozens of bees. "During the war, I saw the vid of you, twelve years old, crawling toward a Mama-Bot like a soldier under barbed wire. It took an hour for you to climb to a tiny hatch midway up her side." He dropped the gloves and cloths into the medkit and sealed it. His free arm went around my middle and he pulled me closer, murmuring into my ear. "You paused and looked back at the ridge where your chapter hid. You said something. No one ever knew what."

"I love you, Pops," I whispered, repeating what I had said that day. "That's why I was doing it. That was all that mattered."

"You were weak, a skinny little thing. And yet your father sent you to the Mama-Bot and directed you to the one hatch we thought you might be able to get in."

"You say we. How were you involved?"

"I was fighting in the Battle of Mobile at the time. We had killed a Mama-Bot the week before. It took a nuke to kill it. We had spotted the hatch, but no one wanted to risk the nanobots. . . ." His voice trailed off. "Your own father sent you into harm's way. Knowing you would come into contact with the PRC mech-nanobots."

I tried to get a deep breath and murmured, "Pliable mode." The suit went limp. I could breathe again. "Yeah. He did. So what? Can we talk about this later?"

"I recognized you the moment I saw you. And I knew that somehow, even with the mech-nanobots, you had survived. For years. You looked tough enough to take me. I've never met a woman who might be able to take me in a fair fight."

"There are no fair fights," I whispered.

"No. There aren't. So . . . how?"

"I was stung. By bicolors."

Jagger went still. His arm tightened around me.

"The male ants swarmed me just outside of a little town, eight weeks before my thirteenth birthday, near the end of the first year of the war. They bit off parts of me, stung me full of poison. Then the queen stung me and deposited me full of DNA-based bio-nanobots."

"People swarmed by bicolors die," he said. "Horribly. I've seen it." In the background, people moved, a fire danced high. Closer, the pump made a steady *erp-slosh* sound, as if it were throwing up. Spy jumped into my lap, sniffed the bloody cloths in the wound kit, and leaped away.

"Three humans survived being stung by a queen,"

I said. "Clarisse Warhammer, me, and a guy. The bio-nanobots attacked me on the genetic level, the way they were designed to do with the ants. They fixed what was wrong with me in the transition, then made alterations they thought I needed to survive. I lived, somehow. I became faster and stronger than pure human.

"And then in the Mama-Bot, I killed some puffers, and a lot of their mech-nanobots got into a cut. My bicolor ant bio-nanobots attacked the new invaders and went to war inside me. I was immediately sick. I was dying and I knew it. But while the nanobots fought it out inside me, I found the Mama-Bot's AI and set a small nuke. I got out. My ant-nanos altered the mech-nanos, and I survived my second transition. It sucked. I remember every feverish, aching, puking moment.

"I was a preadolescent and wasn't able to spread the nanos yet. I was safe for a little while. And the world was safe from me."

"There are all kinds of nanobots," Jagger said.

"Yeah. The bicolor queen's nanos are the only kind that survive inside a human body without taking it apart. If you survive them, they remake you, then attack and take over invader bots. Like me, Cupcake survived nano-transition twice, just like Enrico will have to. You got lucky, in a way. You got my dual bio-mech-nanos on the first try." I laughed, and it was a sad sound. "My fault. And I am so very, *very* sorry."

"So that's what's been making me faster and stronger. Heal faster. All that. Mutated nanos."

It's also what's making you fall in love with me, I thought. But I didn't say it. "I got out of the Mama-Bot, back to OMW base camp. The Mama-Bot died."

"We saw livestream vid. That week, other Mama-Bots were attacked the same way," Jagger said, "and most died, though none of the volunteers survived. I'm guessing because they didn't have bio-nanos to combat the PRC nanos."

"The puffers inside a Mama-Bot carry the nanos

and attack en masse. They'll take a human apart in a skinny hellish minute," I said. My wound itched. That was a bad sign. The PRC nanos were awake and in my wound. "Then the Alien Bugs came; they eventually forced peace on Earth. During all that, puberty hit me. The nanobots did more work, turning me into a Queen. My body changed; the mutated nanos began to secrete through my skin in an attempt to modify others. In an attempt to build a nest."

I'd killed a few people before I started to wear gloves and avoid people. And then Pops got sick. Him I had deliberately infected in an attempt to save him from Parkinson's. But I had waited too long. My nanos couldn't save him.

"My nanobots are changing you," I said, clenching and unclenching my armored fist, remembering the sound of Pops the night he stopped breathing. "I'm sorry. I don't want thralls. I never did." *Though Mateo was clearly not a thrall anymore.* Hope leaped inside me.

"We have a second Antigravity Grabber back at the hotel," Jagger said. "We can decontaminate our suits at least."

On our private channel, Mateo said, "According to my readouts, the PRC mech-nanos came alive in the Simba the moment you banged your head. Mechs last forever and they never die, as long as they have something they can break down and digest. Any nanos you left on the Simba will last seventy-two hours and die off. But any mech-nanos that got into your bloodstream will go to war," Mateo said. "I had hoped that wouldn't happen."

Softly, I said, "So I'm collateral damage to the rescue of Evelyn?" Mateo didn't reply. "*Will* mine die? They infected your spaceship. They turned your AI into Jolene."

"I became Jolene all by myself, sugah," the sentient AI said, breaking into the private chat. "All your little micro-pets did was flip a couple switches before they died off at seventy-two hours. I did all the rest with the ship's libraries: 3D and laser films and vid games and novels. Berger chips gave my CO Mateo back his autonomy and his personality, and I picked a personality all on my own."

On the open channel, Mateo said, "More PRC mech-nanos are waking up. There must be trillions of them. We need the Antigravity Grabber inside the Simba, *now*."

Jagger tapped his comms and said to Amos, "Update."

"I got the water diverted. That motha is one big-assed machine. It's got a path to crawl out of the pit if its batteries get enough charge."

To Jagger, I said, "You better get the hatch open again and drop in the IGP to decontaminate it the way Mateo did the *SunStar*. It can do two jobs at once, charge the engines and kill mech-nanos."

"Use the primary hatch," Mateo said. "The nanos there are still quiescent, and you won't be attacked."

"Roger that," Jagger said.

"I got this," Amos said, the sound of a hatch opening in the background.

From the swamp I heard Amos bellow with joy and then felt the soft vibration of WIMP engines as the Antigravity Grabber powered up the Simba. I smiled slightly and said, "I think the Simba came online."

Into my earbud, Mateo said, "Copy that. Simba. CO Mateo—" That was all I heard before Mateo shut me out of the comm channel.

Jagger slid from beneath me and picked up the sealed wound kit. "I'll toss this into the Simba, under the grabber to decontam." He left me in the cab, his powerful frame throwing night shadows as he walked. I opened a bottle of water and sipped as I watched Gretchen and Cupcake work, feeding the small crowd, putting each of them for a while in the piss-poor medbay. And then Gretchen dragged the first of the still-living attackers close to the fire. Someone threw on fresh logs. The flames danced high.

Cupcake backed away, shock and horror racing through her strongly enough for me to feel traces of it through the nanobots. She whirled away as the man started to scream. Raced for the rig and surged into the cab, shooing me to the passenger side. She started the truck and did a complicated set of maneuvers, getting the rig turned around so it faced outward and we didn't have to watch the fire or the payback. She put music on, something prewar and lighthearted. Loud enough to drown out screams.

I wasn't squeamish, but I was glad not to have to watch or listen. I stared into the night, thinking through what we needed to do before we went after Evelyn. Not for Mateo, but for the rest of the world. We didn't have long.

My nanobots wanted me to have more help. They knew I was about to go into danger, and they wanted their queen in a nest, surrounded by others who would face that threat. But I had never sat back and let others face risk. I had always, every moment of my life, run straight into danger, leading any attack, or, more commonly, taking it on alone. If I had more thralls . . .

I curled my fingers.

I would not make another thrall. I would not.

Except that . . .

Mateo had self-will again. He had created a plan and kept it from me. Mateo was a thrall, but not. Cupcake made her own decisions and had gotten snippy several times on this trip. Thrall, yet not. Jagger may just need more Berger chips. Maybe my thralls would be less slave and more whatever a self-willed thrall was. But I had a feeling they would still want to be around me. I liked being alone. I was a hermit at heart. I didn't want a nest. *Bloody freaking hell.*

I had a lot of thinking to do.

On the far side of the trees, the Simba rolled out of the swamp, over scrub, through mud, and across a small road. It was like watching an entire city block crush across the landscape on tank tracks. Then it stopped. As I watched, Jagger and Amos lowered the portable IGP into the front hatch, resealed it, and climbed down. The Chameleon skin flickered into place, and the traveling lights went dark. Even the noise decreased to nearly nothing beneath Cupcake's bar-hopping, lying, life-is-easy music. Under Mateo's control, the main battle tank had now effectively vanished.

Spy soared to the top of the cab and glared at me through the armored windshield. Without my asking, Cupcake turned the music up to cover the screams, and I opened my door. All the cats raced up, supple as silk, and jumped in. Except Spy. Limber and willowy, she walked across the hood to the open door, holding my gaze as if to make a point. She judged the distance and flew across, twisting in midair, and landed on my lap, an impossible leap-landing. Her claws dug in. She hissed.

"I have armor," I said to her, maybe a tad too complacent.

She hissed again and sprang away. I figured I was doomed. She'd get me back for whatever she was mad about. As long as she didn't hock up a hairball and deposit it on my pillow. I banished that thought and filled my head with images of tins of salmon, just in case she could read my mind. I closed the door. Cupcake turned down the music.

Minutes later, Amos clambered into the back and made himself comfy on his recliner.

Jagger motored up to us on his bike, pointed down the road, and took the lead. Into my earbuds, he said, "I'll call the local Law at dawn with an anonymous tip. Gretchen will turn over the name of Deputy Darson, but not until he's in my hands."

I didn't know what to say to that. "Any of Marconi's men come here?"

Jagger hummed a note that might be an affirmative.

"Listen, Asshole, you can't pretend that sex camp back there didn't happen. Anyone who visited that camp and abused those people—"

"Will be dealt with. Part of the negotiations between Marconi and the OMWs."

"But—"

"None of your business, Shining. I'll handle it."

My thrall had just shut me down. And he wasn't even polite about it.

That was so bloody cool.

An hour outside of Charleston, my armor ran out of power and turned into a rock-hard solid piece of sculpture. It compressed into my middle like a seatbelt combined with an old-fashioned girdle. The pressure instantly made me have to pee, but I had to get out of my armor to do that. Desperate, I ripped one hand free. I lost a little skin. I left behind a little blood at the wrist joint, but the suit would be decontaminated once we got back to the hotel, and Mateo would have to decontam the cab after this trip anyway. The other hand was easier. I didn't bleed on that one.

"What are you doing?" Cupcake asked as we bounced over ruts in the road.

I gave a grunt, lifted a leg up to the dash (which did terrible things to my bladder) and started on my right toes, manually unhinging the armor. The armor resisted. Clearly, I wasn't doing it right, but I was growing frantic.

Spy and her crew took up positions on the dash and stared with intense interest at what I was doing. Occasionally they touched heads one to another. The black male cat thought I'd appreciate how limber he was, so he lifted a leg in the air and cleaned his unneutered privates. Which (again) I did not need to see.

Slowly my leg came free. When I got to my hip, I started twisting and bending in ways my bones were not designed to accommodate. Spy and her clowder thought I was hilarious and made little chuffing noises.

"As soon as I get one arm free, I'll slap all of you," I threatened. That made them chuff harder. Spy showed me her teeth in what communicated clearly, "Try me." It took a lot of work, but I finally got my leg and the necessary parts free of the fancy armor and dragged the rest of me to the composting toilet in back. I tore my undies trying to get them off. "*Bloody damn*," I muttered. The cats gathered around and watched, out of range of my hands or feet. I know. I tried to swat them. But the relief was immediate.

Getting back to my seat, I started working on the other leg. Mildly, Cupcake asked, "Are you trying to get your armor off?"

"What the bloody hell does it look like I'm doing?" I snapped.

"Mmm. Well. See the little silvery disk-shaped thing under either arm? That's a little viber. Press the oval spot in the center with a finger."

I glared at her. Touched the oval spot. Felt the spot shiver a little as the suit compared my identity with the primary initialization. There were little clicks all down my body. The suit fell off me. "You didn't think that might be useful information for me to have?" I demanded.

"You don't like it when we smother you." Cupcake changed gears, slowed, and we bumped over a big rut in the road. I bounced in the seat, nearly banging my head. "It isn't my job to tell you things unless I know you want me to."

I opened my mouth to argue but snapped it shut. She had a point.

"You know how to talk. You can ask," she said.

"You tell her, sugah," Jolene said into the rig's speakers. "All that moping and growling is just a case of bad manners. Yo' mama taught you better."

"You clearly never met Little Mama. She taught me to stand up for myself. And how to throw knives." I wasn't sure where this was going, but some part of me was enjoying the burgeoning argument. *Argument*. My thrall (make that thralls)—Jolene and Cupcake—were arguing with me. *Hallelujah*.

"I bet good green money your mama taught you

to say please and thank you and yes sir and yes ma'am," Jolene said.

"Little Mama wasn't Southern," I said to Jolene.

I tossed my armor behind my seat, found a pair of old pants and work gloves stuffed in a side pocket, dressed, and belted back in. The pants smelled like grease, but what the heck.

"Shame about that. You'd be a lot nicer to deal with if you had been taught to act like a lady."

I burst out laughing, thinking about a lady wearing spike heels and a dainty dress climbing into a Mama-Bot, alone, carrying nothing but a blaster and a tiny nuke to save the world. Yeah. Most ladies had died in the first hours of the war. Those humans who had survived had different skill sets from reading literature, writing poetry, drinking champagne while doing yoga, and ordering around servants. Or whatever ladies did.

The cats were bored and bounded around the cab, finding comfy places to snooze away what was left of the night. Spy jumped into my lap. I waited for her to claw me, but she turned around twice and curled into a ball of purring sweetness. "Faker," I accused her.

We clattered over the bridge. Moments later the hotel came into view. Jagger's people opened the heavy gate to the overflow parking, and Cupcake wheeled the rig and trailer into its spot, which was a lot tighter now that there were all the extra containers taking up space. Jagger and Amos and the two OMW guards went to work setting up the second Antigravity Grabber.

I carried my suit to the grabber, removed the weapons, tossed the armor under the flat surface, checked the AG energy levels, and engaged it. I stripped off the stinky dungarees and gloves and tossed them in too before dressing quickly in the clothes I had discarded forever ago.

My new armor rose into the air and quivered as the energies began to murder the PRC nanobots and my own. Antigravity killed them all. As to the new nanobots inside *me*, well, that should be interesting. Hopefully, I'd be back home to my own pre-set med-bay before they reached critical numbers.

Jagger tossed his suit under the grabber's energies and it rose with mine. Amos and Cupcake were nowhere to be seen. "It's dawn," Jagger said, sticking his fingers into his jeans pockets, thumbs outside. "You want sleep? Or you up for something more entertaining?"

I turned my eyes to his face. He was staring at the armor, his eyes sleepy-looking, but his mouth . . . *Bloody damn.* That mouth. Almost smiling. Relaxed. My belly turned into a pool of molten need. "You know that touching me makes it worse."

He chuckled. "And not touching you is torture."

"I don't want a slave."

"I'm already there, Little Girl. Too little, too late."

I closed my eyes. Hating this. "I need to get the containers back to the scrapyard. There were two women held prisoner at a well-fortified log cabin on the way here. I have a bad feeling they weren't alone, maybe like the people at the campground. I'm going to rescue them and anyone else trapped there. You want to help, get the earthmovers and pumps to Marconi. Hire us rigs to haul the containers. Get us some paid guns. We need to be out of here by midafternoon to get back to the log cabin before dark."

"I'm going with."

"Fine. You can sleep on the way. I got an itchy feeling I need to be back at the med-bay." He looked the question at me. "I'm not feeling so good. The infection is starting sooner than expected."

Jagger cursed and walked away. To do my bidding. Tears pricked my eyes, but I didn't have time for them.

Cupcake and I took care of the gear and secured the decontaminated suits in the shipping container they came in. Exhausted, we trudged to our rooms, showered, and fell into bed.

I woke at 1:00 p.m., alone in the room, shivering

and feverish. Cupcake, her stuff, and the cats were gone. She had laid out my clothes, which she had never done at the scrapyard. I initiated my nearly antique Morphon to find two messages. Mateo had managed to get the Simba to the scrapyard. He had already begun additional decontamination and an electronics sweep, and was running diagnostics on the WIMP engine and the EntNu uplink. Jolene was adding upgrades and connecting the command modules to her systems as backup. And Cupcake was ready to roll. I turned off the Morphon. I doubted anyone could track me on such an old system, but that wasn't a chance I was willing to take.

After a cool shower, sunscreen, and a handful of aspirin, I tossed the sheets, towels, and anything that fit into the tub and filled it with water to kill my nanos. I dressed in the jeans, boots, and two layers of shirts that Cupcake had chosen. Black gloves. Sunglasses, which I especially needed because the transition headache was starting and it was bright outside.

I repacked, hung the Do Not Disturb card on the knob, and left, but paid for four more days, so any remaining nanos would be dead when the room was cleaned. Spy met me in registration and walked me out, tail high, leading the way to the secure parking area where everything was different. There were five rigs now, four hauling the new containers, men and women milling around, all armed. My old rust-bucket was loaded with wooden boxes I recognized from Marty's, and covered with my old cheap scrap.

Jacopo Marconi was standing beside Jagger, a duffel at his feet, and his brother Enrico was trussed up, gagged, blindfolded, and sitting on the cracked asphalt. The cats were hiding under my rig in the shade. Cupcake was giving directions and instructions to the drivers and hired guns. I wasn't needed, so I walked to Enrico and placed my palms on his face. I pushed with my blood, with my nanobots, beginning the transition that would make him mine. Or kill him. By the time we got back to the scrapyard, he would be ready for the med-bay.

When I stood, I spotted Jagger. He was weaponed up like a space cowboy, wearing yesterday's clothes, hadn't shaved, had sweat rings under his arms and down his back, and *bloody hell*, he looked good. The moment I thought that, he looked up and met my eyes, holding my gaze. There was a lot of heat in that stare for a moment, and then he blinked, and it was gone. That was good, right? It had to be good that he could shut it down. He said, "Deputy Darson was gone. Marconi has people looking for him."

"Okay. Will he keep us informed?"

"He'll tell his kid." He inclined his head to Jacopo and said to him, "You ride with Amos in a rig. Part way there you'll be blindfolded. Your brother rides with me in another rig. Bikes are loaded for later travel." Louder, to the drivers and guards, he said, "Let's roll!"

In seconds we were ready to go, and five rigs rumbled to life. I climbed painfully into my cab, ignoring the cats who jumped in through the open door. Belting myself in, I stretched out my legs, my joints aching, and propped them on the dash. Shifting like the pro she was, Cupcake maneuvered out of the lot, leading the way for the convoy.

She passed me an electrolyte drink, which was slimy and nasty, but I drank it down as we pulled out of Charleston and left behind the last bit of green and civilization I'd see for a while. Of course, civilization had included a sex-slave camp, so maybe not so civilized.

As the last of the farms disappeared, Cupcake glanced at me side-eyed and said, "I know you're dying and all, but we're still going to clean out the sex-ring log cabin and kick some butt on the way home, right?"

I shivered, my teeth clattering, knowing it was the fever rising, and while I wanted to be under a blanket, that would only make matters worse. Cupcake passed me a bag of ice and said, "Hold it behind your neck. And answer my question."

I was sure I hadn't told Cupcake about my fears for the women there. Had the cats told her? Were they talking to her too, mind-to-mind? That was terrifying, but I was too sick to address that possibility. "Sure. We'll kick some ass. Bonus points if there's an e-trail showing a tie to the military, Deputy Darson, the MS Angels, the Law, or the Gov. If it is a sex shop, that's too coincidental for there not to be a link."

"Hey, Jolene," Cupcake said. "You hear the boss lady? Get cracking."

"Sugah, I been on that since y'all left that place."

"Good," I said. "I'm going to the sleeper cab to rest." I unbelted, shoved cats out of the way, crawled into the back, lowered the foldup bed, and fell onto the bare mattress, holding the ice against my middle now. I dropped into oblivion.

I woke when the cab fell silent, the constant rumble gone. I was on my side, wrapped around the still-cool water bag, sweating. The fever had temporarily broken, but I was weak, aching, and even breathing hurt.

Spy was curled into the crook of my arm, purring. Other cats were behind my knees, against my back, one against my head. I grunted, Spy awoke, and the others came awake too. Shoving cats away, I sat up. There was a tiny comms system, two bottles of electrolyte drink, four aspirin, and an energy bar I recognized as coming from the *SunStar* on the tiny fold-out table. Seemed Cupcake's inventory of my scrapyard had included the spaceship. No wonder she and Jolene were cozy.

I drank the drinks, took the aspirin, and ate the bar. It was tasteless, but I needed the calories. When I could stand, I stepped across the cat litter box and used the cab toilet. Everything in the cab stank because of my toxic sweat. There was a tiny portable body wand I could use to clean myself, but it would take a lot of time, and I could hear voices outside. Cupcake. Jagger. Amos. Jacopo. No engines anywhere.

I breathed deep despite the pain, palmed the comms system, braced myself, and stepped from the cab, the cats landing all around me.

The first thing I saw was the eight-person donning unit, some sections with armor already in place. In neat rows were the wooden boxes I had seen packed on the flatbed back at the hotel, the wooden boxes from the first container I had opened at Marty's. Their lids were off. Two of them I remembered, each holding three long rifles capable of multiple-caliber projectiles, all with AI targeting and high-capacity mags. A box of hand weapons was beside it. In organized rows were crates of ammo—the various calibers that would fit the weapons. Last was a case of third-gen blasters, RADR IIIs—pretty, sleek, with armor neural-link capability. They probably had greater range and improved lethality than the one I had killed Marty with.

I walked on around the now-empty rig, trying to figure out where I was. There was a creek in a half-dry riverbed off to the side of the cracked, broken road. It looked a lot like what was left of Big Coal River and Coal River Road, just outside Sylvester, a few klicks from where the log cabin was.

My crew stood under the shade of a tree: Amos, Cupcake, Jacopo, Jagger. They stopped talking and looked me over. They could probably smell me even through the distance that separated us.

The comms system, a tiny thing the size of my pinkie fingernail, vibrated. I tucked it into my ear, and Mateo said, "Afternoon. Cupcake says you're sick."

"Yeah. What do you care?"

"You'll survive. You always have."

My heart clenched at the callous response. "Update," I demanded, not crossing the distance to the small group.

"The Simba needs a test run before we go after Evelyn. Cupcake said you intend to close down the armored log cabin and rescue the prisoners. And yeah, Jolene and I've been checking it out since you left. Sat-sensors say it's full of prisoners."

I said nothing.

"So I got us into place on a low hillock, two klicks from the building, which is another two klicks from your current location."

"Us?"

"Simba, Jolene, and me."

"Hey there, sugah. Soon as you're in your suit, I can monitor your vitals and stick you full of meds to compensate for the transition."

I grunted softly.

"And the suit's got a full power load this time, Sweet Thang, so you can make comprehensive use of the complete armor tech and weapons capability."

Mateo said, "We can do a trial run of our plan to take down Warhammer."

"And the others?" I asked, staring at the group under the tree, knowing the answer already. "What do they say about it?"

"They're in."

All this for Evelyn. All this planning. All these machinations behind my back. I wanted to lash out at Mateo. I wanted to hurt him as badly as he was hurting me. But . . .

I remembered the sight of him the day I rescued him from the small-town sheriff who had enslaved him as his own personal bullyboy and computer. The mess he had been when I got him to the office and out of the warbot suit. The PRC nanos had eaten him, piece by piece.

All I had wanted for years was for Mateo to be his own man, not a thrall to me. I just hadn't expected him to betray me when that day came. I hadn't expected it to hurt. Sometimes getting what you want is painful. "What do your sensors say about the armaments?"

"The walls have minimal exterior armor; appear to be standard prewar build of logs and plaz-crete. However, I'm detecting something on the inside, maybe carbon-fiber reinforcement. Windows are reinforced—old-style bullet-resistant glass, not silk-plaz—

but will stand up to anything except the Simba's bigger weapons. Garage doors are reinforced with graphite epoxy trusses and hemp-plaz carbon-fiber composite, possibly scavenged from a black-market Tesla fuselage. One mid-war laser cannon visible from above the left garage door, possibly also from a Tesla.

"I count"—he hesitated—"twelve distinct humans on the second floor. Twenty-seven on the main floor, but one room is heavily packed, and I can't differentiate exact numbers. Likely a prisoners' dormitory.

"Eleven vehicles are out front: four armored Supra-El utility vehicles; the two tanks you took down before; four motorbikes; and one county car, possibly Hand of the Law. Lot of people moving with purpose."

Darson? I wondered. It would make sense for him to flee from one sex shop to another.

Watching the group who were watching me, I considered that information. Turned on a heel and walked off to the side, toward the river. "Describe the bikes."

"Two Harleys, two LPMs, newer models, maybe last five years."

"Black and blue and green-flame paint jobs?"

"Negative. Solid black. Why do you ask." It was a demand, the tone of a spaceship CO talking to his subordinate.

"Spy spotted some motorbikes while we were in Charleston, and she was upset by them, but they looked different." I sat on a rock at the water's edge. The creek was a steady trickle, the sound of moving water rare these days, except when storms blew through. "There was a deputy's car at the log cabin when we came through last time. Any chance the county car is Darson's?"

"The vehicle is parked at the wrong angle for me to be sure. Do I need to work my way in closer?"

"Hold your position." As an afterthought, I added, "Please."

I pulled off my glove and put my fingers in the water. It was warmer than body temp and sludgy with algae. "Jolene? Did you find a paper trail on Darson's finances?"

"It's incomplete, sugah, but he only showed up in Charleston two years ago, so his financial backtrail is short. However, he lives in a mighty fine house in Charleston for a county Hand of the Law, and he has a partnership in a string of strip clubs from St. Louis to Louisville." *Strip clubs* was a euphemism for the sex trade.

St. Louis to Louisville was the direction the MS Angels had been moving the last time Harlan and I talked. St. Louis was one of their biggest strongholds. Nothing about the sex shops was coincidence.

"Any sign the rest of the sheriff's office personnel are living higher on the economic ladder than their salaries indicate should be possible?"

"Negative," Jolene said. "Don't mean they ain't hidin' the money better than Darson, though."

I nodded to myself and mentally called Spy. She raced up and sat on my thighs. I tilted my head forward, asking her to touch mine. The world tilted and I wanted to vomit, but I held it in. I told her what I wanted. She hissed and backed away, nearly flying to a rock nearby, her tail twitching in either excitement or anger. Hard to tell which.

I pulled on my glove and walked back to the group, saying to Mateo, "Send the GPS to Cupcake's Morphon." I tapped off the comms. "Gear up. We're taking the log cabin." And it needed to be soon, because I could feel the shivers getting close again.

"'Bout damn time," Cupcake said.

I stripped off the boots and pants and stepped up to the donning station. I initiated it, closed my eyes, and prepared for misery, because this time, I needed to allow full hookup, even the private parts. And it would not be pleasant.

Running four kilometers—weaponed up and carrying two cats—was nothing while wearing fully charged, restocked armor in full battle mode, even with me sick as a dog. It was late afternoon by the time we had positioned ourselves and were ready to initiate the plan devised by Mateo and me, one that included the cats. Spy, wearing a tiny camera secured on her chest and tied directly into our face shields, leaped from my arms, followed by the other cats, and raced for the house. I settled myself, sitting against a tree trunk, eyes closed, to follow her through the mental link we had established before we left the scrapyard.

The world shuddered and shook, and I wanted to hurl. Instead, my body stabilized and relaxed. According to my suit monitor, Jolene had taken over my armor and was injecting a combo of meds based on the transition protocol of the med-bay in the scrapyard's office.

"Okay, Spy," I murmured. Feeling oddly tranquil, I reached for the explorer cat, found her, and saw through her eyes.

Spy was perched in a tree, the limb overlooking the western gable of the log cabin. From this vantage, she could see the front of the house, the garages, and had a clear view of the parking area. Into my comms system, I said, "The tanks are being repaired. There are multiple mechanics and weapons specialists working on them."

Spy showed me other visions as well, one at a time, which kept the nausea and vertigo at bay, though I got the feeling that she found it silly that I couldn't see all seven cat visions at once. Each view was from a different outside perspective, and I told the other humans the positions of the guards before Spy turned her attention inside the windows.

Inside the front window, a woman once again danced on a pole in front of a group of men. I counted the men. All were armed. All wore gray camo fatigues, the same kind I remembered from the sex-shop camp. My fears had been right.

The high-level MS Angels wore gray camo. Had ever since the war. One of the men we squished on the way to Charleston had worn washed-out black camo. I hadn't thought about it at the time since gray camo was common enough in the backcountry among West Virginia hunters. I hadn't caught it until I saw the dead men at the camp.

"Mateo. They're wearing MS Angels camo, just like some of the men at the campground. Jagger had to have noticed, and he didn't say anything about that."

Mateo hesitated, and finally settled on, "Good for him."

I blew out a breath. Jagger knew stuff he wasn't telling me. More evidence my hold on him wasn't complete. So . . . yeah. Good.

Through a different window and the eyes of a different cat, I saw what looked like a dormitory or a barracks, bunk beds everywhere, men sleeping on some, others vacant, all the linens filthy, gray camo hanging haphazardly here and there. Another window showed a woman administering meds to another woman. A guard held a weapon on them. There was a door with a deadbolt in the background. No one put a deadbolt inside a house unless it was to keep weapons or valuables safe or hold prisoners. I had no idea how many more secure doors were in the place.

In the back of the house on the second story I saw an office that was set up like a hunting lodge, lots of taxidermied animal heads on the wood-paneled walls. Leather chairs. Six men sat around a table, playing cards. Half were wearing neat gray camo and the others were dressed in expensive clothes. The clean clothing, the cigars, the liquor in crystal glasses said these were the men I was looking for.

"Jolene, put up a pic of Deputy Darson."

I opened my eyes to see a digital of the deputy on my faceplate. *Gotcha, you piece of garbage.*

"Darson is on premises, second story, rear of the building. Six men in one room. It has a view of the far side of the hill the house is perched on. He's with the . . ." I stopped and started laughing.

"What?" Jagger demanded.

"You remember the intel that the president of the MS Angels went running from Warhammer? He's here. Guess what, Jagger? You get to take out the OMW's worst enemy, Rico "Three Fingers" Garcia Perez."

Jagger said nothing.

"That means this cabin is more fortified than my sensors show," Mateo said.

I sent Spy a message vision instructing her to find a way inside. "Let's see where the prisoners are," I whispered to the cat. Spy slithered to the ground and into the shadows. The black male cat followed. They slipped in through an open window.

Mateo said, "Got a glimpse of good shielding on Spy's camera beneath the wallboard. Might be military stuff."

Visions of the house showed filthy back rooms. The kitchen was a horror. A communal bathroom was unspeakable, and Spy let me know that humans were disgusting and needed to be taught how to use a litterbox.

Spy and the black cat slinked silently through the house, sniffing things I was glad I couldn't smell. They glided up and down stairs, investigating rooms where they could, bypassing areas with too many people or too many closed doors.

"You getting this, Mateo?" I asked.

"Affirmative. Floor plans underway."

I described what I had seen of the house from the cats' vantages. On a small area of my faceplate, floor plans came into view. "Nice," I said. "Mateo, points of entry?"

"We need to know where the two women in the front room end up when the shooting starts. See if the cats can find a secure position outside that room but with visual on the doors."

"Okay." I sent Spy a request while Mateo, the wartime CO, gave orders.

"We fire on three. Jagger, Cupcake. When I say

the word, take out the armed guards in front and start picking off anyone who reaches for a weapon. Amos, get into position in back and eliminate the guard on the hillside. Jacopo, you say you can shoot. Take the guard on the left of the house. That's a tricky shot. I've got the heavy weapons. I'm set to take out the cannon and eradicate the garage doors, the front door, and, if the women are gone, the main front window."

"Roger that," we all said.

"Once the enemy combatants are down out front, Cupcake and Jacopo, you cover the outside and the driveway. Amos enters from the back, Jagger from the front door or window, whichever comes down first. Smith," he said, meaning me, to keep my name from Jacopo, on the off-chance he didn't already know it, "you go through the garage doors. Keep all positional monitors active so I can coordinate if needed."

"Roger that," Cupcake said.

"Send in the cats," Mateo said.

"All cats go," I whispered to Spy. "Find the prisoners. Disable their guards."

I had a view of more cats leaping through the open window.

"OK. On three," Mateo said. "One."

I slammed down my face shield. Jolene shot me full of battle chemicals. My heart raced. Breathing deepened. My suit fed me higher oxygen levels.

"Two."

I stood, activated the armor's antirecoil and hardening features.

"Three."

The barrage started.

The laser cannon poking out of the building took a direct hit and exploded. Logs, splinters, and shielding flew.

The armed men out front died.

The garage doors blew apart, Tesla shielding flying. Decapitating a man aiming into the woods.

I raced toward the house. Men in gray camo began to fall.

I sped across the open parking area. Ducked under flying debris.

The workers who reached for weapons were picked off behind me.

The workers who cowered and rolled under vehicles were spared. For now.

I ducked inside. Shotgun in hand. Two bodies slumped against the back wall. Hamburger.

Form in the doorway. Gray camo. Weapon. I fired. He slid down the wall.

I advanced, took out three more. Then more. "Garage clear. Entry hallway to the house, clear. All the men from the front room ran this way. All down."

"Sending out two female prisoners. Hold fire," Jagger said. A moment later, he said, "Front room clear." From inside the house a shot fired. Another. "Hallway clear left and right. Stairway to upper level, clear," Jagger said.

"Back entrance, clear," Amos said. "Heading up back stairs."

I stumbled forward. Dizzy, disoriented. Shivering. Transition sickness combined with the vision of seven cats as they sped toward two guards who were entering a room. The cats threw themselves upon the men. Claws cutting, fangs biting, screeching. I fell against a wall.

Two women in the room attacked the men too. My cat-sight resolved into one set of eyes, Spy's. A white-haired woman took a weapon from a guard and put two shots into his head. Two shots into the other one. Two women in front of the group were now armed and clearly had training. The other women were staring at the bodies and cats.

Some cats sped away, back down the hall, following Spy's order, which was a visual of coyotes. Confusing, until I realized she was calling the men wild dogs and ordering her cats to watch and attack.

Spy stood atop one dead body, made eye contact with the white-haired woman, and hissed. It was a "follow me" command. Spy leaped out the door, looked back, and hissed again. The woman opened her mouth, shocked, and said, "I think we just got rescued by a bunch a cats. Carol, you're the best shot. At our six. Let's move." Spy sped down the hallway following the black male cat. Cats zigged and zagged. Clearing the rooms. Sounding alarms.

"The women are heading toward the back stairs," I said. "Cats leading."

My sensors showed movement. I shoved upright, turned toward the shape. Almost fired, until I saw the pink. *Amos*.

He discharged a shot off to my left, and a body fell. "Hell yeah," he said. "This is fun!" He whirled, and took off, shouting, "I got the back stairs. I'll take the women into the woods."

"Where are the men from the upstairs lounge?" I asked into comms.

All I got back was the sound of Jagger clearing rooms and firing.

Amos called out to the women. "I'm with the fucking cats! This way!"

"Amos. Six men, the top brass, somewhere in the house."

"Amos. Stop on the stairs," a young voice said, the words sharp. "A hidden door opened on the back of the house. Six men. Three in MS Angels camo." *Jacopo. Good tactical awareness, maneuvering to cover the back.* "All heavily armed," he said. "There's two Outlander Vehicles. Take all of the men out?"

"Make sure the MSAs are all taken out," I said. "I want the deputy alive, but I don't care if he's in good shape or not."

Shots rang out.

A sensor pinged. A blow hit my back. I'd been shot. It hurt. I pivoted. Fired. Again. Again. Again. Changed out magazines as two bodies fell.

"All down," Jacopo said, calmly. "Deputy needs a knee-replacement med-bay. Others need caskets."

"Jagger," I asked. "House clear?"

"Roger that. All clear."

"Get the women out," I said.

"Covering the back of the house as the prisoners are exfil'ed," Jacopo said. "Will target and take out anything else that moves."

"Got it, Marconi," Amos said. "Let's go, ladies."

I walked to the front room and looked out the busted window. Discovered that all the men outside were dead except for one. Cupcake strode to him and shot him in the head. Cupcake was scary.

I moved through the house and out the back. I swiveled and studied the house. Far as I could tell, there was no damage to the log wall. Jacopo hadn't missed. He was scary too.

Darson was lying on his side, moaning. I walked to him and kicked him flat. I relaxed the suit hardening and squatted beside him. Shoved up my face shield and gave him my scariest smile. "Hey. I need info. Your only chance to live is to tell me everything." He rolled his head side to side, moaning. I thought about the women in the campground. The women here. I pulled off a glove and held my hand above his neck. Warhammer's nanobots were all through him. I could feel the vibrations of the nanos in his flesh, in his blood, just as I had felt Marty's contagion.

I regloved and said, casually, "You were going to take out the head of the MS Angels for her, weren't you? And then Marconi. Talk to me or die."

He groaned and shook his head no.

"That was your one and only chance. You won't die easy," I said.

I stood and looked at the others. "Toss him into the truck bed. Jacopo. Tell your father that he just inherited a house. It's a little beat up, but it can be reno'ed."

Jagger looked as if he was going to argue for OMW territory, so I added, "Tell him it's a gift from the OMW." Jagger started laughing.

"Thank you, Ms. Smith. I'm sure my father will be appropriately appreciative."

I wasn't sure what that meant, but I'd take the

win. "Let's get the women treated and dressed. Make sure they have money and trade goods and a way out of here." I checked the time and was shocked to see that the battle had lasted a total of fourteen minutes. Seemed like forever.

Jagger and Amos made the trip to the scrapyard on bikes liberated from the log cabin. Jacopo, blindfolded and loosely bound, sat in Amos's dirty recliner. Cupcake drove and didn't sing, thankfully. I was feverish, sick, sleeping on the foldout bed with the cats, the odor of the litterbox not helping my nausea. My fever was high enough that Cupcake kept stopping the rig and changing out my ice bags with fresh ice she had taken from the log cabin. Wasting water on me. I got a case of giggles thinking about that, but I had no idea why it was funny. Delirious maybe.

We got to the junkyard in the middle of the night, and found the other rigs parked out front, drivers asleep inside each, the hired armed guards sitting in strategic places. Mateo's security measures had kept the drivers and hired guns out. Our secrets were still secure. The cats raced from the cab and disappeared, probably to share their experiences with the others. I sat on the ground at the entrance and leaned against the pillar that hid weaponry. I was shaking so hard I thought I might rattle my brains. My temp was really high. I needed the med-bay, but I had things to take care of.

Cupcake displaced the guards and the drivers, tossed Enrico to the ground from where he had been sleeping in one of the cabs, then drove each of the rigs into the scrapyard and deposited the containers at the back near the *SunStar*. The empty rigs drove off, leaving Jagger, Cupcake, Amos, Enrico (still trussed up like a turkey), Jacopo (who was now allowed to see what little there was to see in the dark), Darson, and me. I noted that the sign advertising the scrapyard was down. Mateo, thinking ahead, had removed it.

Cupcake gave Jacopo a pair of gloves and made sure he put them on securely. "Daddy wanted you to see the med-bay," she said. "Come on." They walked into the dark.

Jagger unloaded two more matte-black motorbikes from my rig. I hadn't noted him taking them at the log cabin. Smart man. Cupcake reappeared soon after, took Jacopo's gloves, and poured some precious water into a basin. She dropped in the gloves. "Step in," she directed him. He did. "Stomp around some," she added. He looked incredulous but followed the order.

Smart woman. Killing my nanobots.

"Get on the bike," she ordered. "You'll leave when Jagger does." Jacopo shrugged a lot like his father had and straddled the bike. He clearly thought we were all deranged.

Jagger and Jacopo waited outside the gates, Jagger keeping his charge safe from my nanobots. Cupcake grabbed Darson's collar and dragged him into the night. The screams started instantly, but before he cut comms, I heard Mateo say, "You don't need that thumb. Tell me where Warhammer is." He'd find where the other queen was. Where Evelyn was. I felt no pity at all.

Cupcake walked back to the entrance, her skirt swishing. She had changed into a frilly dress, which was weird.

"I want in," Amos said, before I could even start talking. "You need a guy like me. I like cats. I like junk. I like fighting. And I like Cupcake."

I felt Cupcake flush. Bloody hell. She liked Amos. As in *liked*. "Walk with us," I said. I held up my hand and Cupcake pulled me to my feet. We three walked away from Jagger and Jacopo. I said, "This isn't a short-term job, Amos. I'm sick. Think of it like a type of plague. You stay, you *will* get sick. When you get well, you will never want to leave. You will *never leave*," I emphasized. "Smith's Junk and Scrap is in the middle of nowhere, in the West Virginia desert. Closest town is Naoma, which is where you'll have to bunk until I heal Enrico."

"Will I infect other people?"

"No."

He pursed his mouth and moved his jaw side to side, as if thinking. "Fine. Long as I can't infect people. I packed all my gear and turned in the keys on my rental. I'm staying."

"We're going to war soon, and you don't even know why. This isn't your fight."

He waved a hand in the air as if flapping away something stinky. "I'm good with all that shit on one condition. If Cupcake would consider having dinner with me tonight."

"Me?" she squeaked.

"Sexiest thang I ever saw in my life was you in that armor targeting an enemy and takin' 'em out, one by one. I'd be honored to buy you a steak as big as Texas."

"There's only one restaurant in Naoma. I'm wearing a dress," she bargained, "meaning wine, not beer, and no peanuts on the floor."

"I'll pick you up an hour before sunset. In a car. And I'll have flowers."

"Flowers?" She looked at me and said, "Holy shit. What am I supposed to do with flowers?"

Jolene interrupted. "Put them in a vase with water and every time you see 'em, think of the great guy who brought them to you."

"What she said," Amos said.

"Okay," I said, knowing I would be making another thrall, but not seeing a way out of it and honestly too sick to really care. "You're hired. Cupcake. Send his Morphon directions to the boardinghouse in Naoma. Make arrangements for a room there." I had never said those words. But I had trade goods, cash, and jewels. Financially, I wasn't hurting for the first time in my life. "And Cupcake, you know where to deposit Enrico."

"Got it. I'll see you tonight," Cupcake said to

Amos, punching info into her Morphon. "And remember. No peanuts." With a little wave, she hauled Enrico off, and Amos puttered away into the dark on one of the appropriated motorbikes. Jagger motioned Jacopo to stay with the bikes and cut comms. I cut mine, leaving Jagger and me alone in the night.

I studied the OMW enforcer, wondering what my latest transition would do to him. To us. "What did McQuestion say about Jacopo?"

"I put Marconi and him in contact. McQuestion negotiated an arrangement with Marconi. Marconi gets his daughter in exchange for Jacopo."

"Mutual hostages," I said, thinking about an OMW daughter sitting beside Mina at Marconi's dinner table. I wondered how long it would it be before the assassin shoved a pencil through her temple into her brain. I shook the thought away.

"What about us?" Jagger asked.

"I'm sick. There may *be* no us. You might be free of our nanobot connection after this transition."

"Nanobots or no," he said, giving me a half smile, "we got something between us."

"You're the enforcer. You don't get to have relationships outside the OMW."

"Little Girl, there are ways. It's been done before." He stepped to me and enclosed me in his arms. He felt cool against my feverish skin. He kissed me gently, as if aware that my chapped lips hurt. "Contact me when you find Warhammer. I'm part of your war now."

"We'll see how you feel after this transition," I said. "Meantime, let me go. I got things to do. A war to plan."

Jagger couldn't resist a direct order. He backed away. Which broke my heart.

"Take Jacopo through back roads until he's lost and can't find his way here. Then you and he go to McQuestion and deal with this little hostage situation. Go do the OMW thing; be the enforcer and his little crack-shot Hells Angels sidekick."

Jagger cursed and walked into the dark. I heard two bikes start up, one a Harley, one a Kawasaki. They too motored into the dark, heading in a direction away from Naoma. My heart breaking, my steps unsteady, I walked to the office. Enrico was blindfolded, still bound, and leaning against the office when I stooped and placed my hands on his face again. I pushed with my blood and my nanobots, speeding his transition.

For days, Cupcake and Amos moved Enrico and me back and forth, from the med-bay to my bed, keeping us stabilized and giving Enrico intensive—very intensive—Berger-chip treatments throughout his transition, a timing and intensity I hadn't tried. It was Cupcake's idea all the way, Old Man Marconi's chosen chips teaching Enrico about Italy—the historic, pre-World War III Italy—and how to speak Italian.

At the end of the first three days, I climbed from the med-bay and, while I wasn't great, I was okay-ish. Enrico, who had been blindfolded the entire time, was ready to go home, though he was a very altered, very Italian Enrico, who had forgotten how to speak English. Marconi might not like that part, but the intensive chip therapy seemed to have drastically lessened Enrico's attachment to anyone. Which was amazing.

Now that I was stable, Amos was in the med-bay, learning via chip how to maintain all the equipment in the scrapyard and how to fly a high-altitude, low-orbit WIMP engine fighter jet, which he had always wanted to learn. He and Cupcake had clearly spent the last days growing closer, a lot closer, and she cast loving glances at Amos before she took off, driving the still-blindfolded Enrico to a mutually agreed upon safe place for Marconi to pick him up.

For the first time in ages, I had the office to myself. Well, as much to myself as the giant of a man in the med-bay allowed.

Alone, I drank a cup of coffee and grieved Harlan,

because that was what vengeance was for. Then I walked into the morning sun, Spy and the black cat on my heels. I realized that the black cat hadn't been brought for neutering. So that meant . . . he and Spy were like the male fighter cats and the older queens. Okay. Good to know who the next generation of cat leaders would be. I'd have to figure out what to call him.

I wandered through the scrapyard, seeing all the changes Cupcake had made while I was confined to the med-bay. Smith's had been organized chaos when I took it over, and that had remained my style through the years. Cupcake had different ideas, and the place looked good.

Tapping my comms, I said, "Mateo. You around?"

"Affirmative. Your two o'clock."

I turned right and stopped. In the middle of the aisle was a corpse, recently dead, the blood still fresh. Darson. He had been dismembered. The cats were gathered around, feeding, eating the protein. Spy sauntered up beside Tuffs and crouched. They touched noses before Spy helped herself to some fresh liver.

"You know where Warhammer is?" I asked into comms.

"Yeah. I know all sorts of things."

"Like what?"

Mateo's warbot raised high, an aisle over, his form unfolding, his chameleon skin going pearlized gray. He tilted his spider-like carapace, towering over me. His eyes focused into mine through the plaz-silk window. He looked angry and tired and, very oddly, beaten. "I'm less tied to you," he said.

"Good." That seemed to surprise him, so I added, "I never wanted you as a thrall. I just wanted to save you."

He watched the cats eating his victim, then said, "Warhammer and Evelyn are in a wartime military bunker at the intersection of old I-77 and I-81, near Fort Chiswell. We'll need backup to take her down.

None of the plans we discussed will work."

"Okay. I'm here for you. Your war is my war."

Mateo blinked. "You could have done what Warhammer is doing. You could have raised an army. Taken over the world."

I laughed, the sound too loud in the empty junkyard. The cats all stopped and looked at me, then went back to eating. "And have to rule? *Bloody hell*, Mateo. I got a junkyard to run. I don't have time for stupid stuff like running the world. Besides. The Bugs are probably still here, hiding somewhere. They'll take out anyone using the wrong weapons. This isn't our world anymore."

"But it could be."

I thought about that. "Nah. I don't want it. I'm going back to the office to check on Amos and eat lunch. I hear you and Cupcake have watermelon sprouting."

Mateo shook his misshaped head. "I'll never understand you."

"I may not be the active Little Girl, anymore, Mateo, but I'm still OMW, and Pops's daughter. The world doesn't interest me. I got what I want here."

"What you 'got here' is a bunch of junk and a Bug ship, Shining. And the *SunStar*."

"Yeah. Later."

I wandered to the greenhouse to pick some fresh produce. Maybe have a beer or two.

It was a good day to be alive.

About the Author

Faith Hunter is a New York Times and USA Today bestselling author. She writes dark urban fantasy, paranormal urban thrillers, paranormal police procedurals, and science fiction.

Her long-running, bestselling, Skinwalker series features Jane Yellowrock, a hunter of rogue-vampires. The Soulwood series features Nell Nicholson Ingram in paranormal crime solving novels. Her Rogue Mage novels, a dark, post-apocalyptic fantasy series, features Thorn St. Croix, a stone mage in an alternate reality. She also writes a Scifi novella series: Junkyard Cats.

Under the pen name Gwen Hunter, she has written action adventure, mysteries, thrillers, women's fiction, a medical thriller series, and even historical religious fiction. As Gwen, she was part of the WH Smith Literary Award for Fresh Talent in the UK, and won a Romantic Times Reviewers Choice Award in 2008. Under all her pen names, she has over 40 books in print in 30 countries. Faith has won numerous awards and *Curse on the Land* won an Audie Award for 2017.

In real life, Faith once broke a stove by refusing to turn it on for so long that its parts froze and the unused stove had to be replaced. She collects orchids and animal skulls, rocks and fossils, loves to sit on the screened back porch in lightning storms, and is a workaholic with a passion for whitewater kayaking and RV travel. She prefers Class III whitewater rivers with no gorge to climb out of, and drinks a lot of tea.

Some days she's a lady. Some days she ain't.

www.faithhunter.net   www.gwenhunter.com
www.facebook.com/official.faith.hunter

Made in United States
Troutdale, OR
09/14/2023